I LIKE
TO WATCH

Christopher Pierce is the editor of *Biker Boys: Gay Erotic Stories* (Cleis Press) and the author of *Kidnapped by a Sex Maniac: The Erotic Fiction of Christopher Pierce*. Visit him online at christopherpierceerotica.com.

I LIKE
TO WATCH
GAY EROTIC STORIES

EDITED BY
CHRISTOPHER PIERCE

Published in the United States by Cleis Press Inc., 2246 Sixth Street, Berkeley, California 94710.

Printed in the United States.
Cover design: Scott Idleman/Blink
Cover photograph: Jack Slomovits/Getty Images
Text design: Frank Wiedemann
Cleis logo art: Juana Alicia
First Edition.
10 9 8 7 6 5 4 3 2 1

ISBN: 978-1-57344-422-4

Contents

INTRODUCTION

E ver since my high school wrestling teammate found me jerking off with his jockstrap on my head after a meet and instead of beating the crap out of me, told me to finish so he could watch, I've been fascinated with the symbiotic fetishes I later learned were called *exhibitionism* and *voyeurism*.

Having sex alone or with others is often stimulating enough, but the extra thrill of watching or being watched (or both at the same time) adds the perfect element to the mix, like a certain seasoning that elevates a dish that is merely delicious into the realm of the sublime.

When I was awarded the privilege of editing a gay voyeur/exhibitionist collection for Cleis Press, I knew I had a tough act to follow. Erotic literary mistresses Alison Tyler and Rachel Kramer Bussel's brilliant 2006 collection *Caught Looking* set the bar high for this kind of book, and I have endeavored to live up to its legacy. I don't have space to praise each story in *I Like to Watch*, though they all deserve accolades, but there are several I particularly hope to whet your appetite with:

Longtime favorite Jeff Mann's "Good Boy" is achingly erotic and heart wrenching at the same time.

Gregory L. Norris's masterpiece, "The Rookie," aside from providing the heart and core of *I Like To Watch*, is a fantastic exploration of how a fetish can transcend itself and become a life-changing force in a man's life.

Special guest Simon Sheppard's "God's Own Exhibitionist" is as literary and crotch grabbing as we've come to expect from his boundless talent and imagination.

I hope you find the stories I've collected (almost) as arousing as actually watching or being watched.

Don't close your blinds tonight!

Christopher Pierce

REPRIEVE

Michael Bracken

After the sun slipped behind the high-rise horizon and the street below me became littered with neon and incandescent light, I knelt on the flat tar-paper roof of an old warehouse turned office building, leaned against the waist-high brick parapet and peered through the scope of my high-powered rifle. My target's apartment was half a floor lower than my vantage point, at the southwest corner of a building four blocks away. I examined the interior of the apartment through the bedroom window and through the sliding glass door that separated the balcony from the living room, admiring the decorator's taste until Kevin Foreman stepped from the bathroom wearing nothing but a bulging blue jockstrap sparkling with silver glitter.

My finger tightened on the trigger. I could have taken Foreman out right then, but he suddenly grabbed a white terry-cloth robe from the bed and slipped into it as he hurried from the bedroom and through the living room. He paused, tied the sash, ran his fingers through his damp blond hair to push it behind his ears and seemed to take a deep breath to calm himself. Then he opened the apartment door and greeted the man standing on the other side. I wouldn't know what either man was saying until I had an unobstructed view of their faces and could read their lips, but I could make assumptions about them from their appearance.

The two men were quite a contrast. From what I had seen when he stepped out of the bathroom and before he had pulled on the robe, Foreman had the body of a naturally slender man gone soft, neither overweight nor well toned, a light all-over tan, and he kept his face and pretty much everything else from his neck down clean shaven. The man filling the doorway was several years older than Foreman, with a granite jaw covered by a dark, post–five o'clock shadow, a square face the color and texture of worn leather and closely cropped black hair sprinkled heavily with salt at the temples. He wore a navy-blue, single-breasted suit jacket over his thick chest, a crisp button-down white shirt and a red tie still knotted at the neck this late in the evening. Sharply creased trousers that matched the jacket led down to black Oxfords shined to a high gloss, and the only jewelry I could see was a gold band on his left ring finger. The scar on his right cheek, the probable result of a close encounter with a knife during his youth, told me more about him than he would have expected. He was much like the men who usually hired me.

Foreman moved aside as his visitor stepped into the apartment. After my target closed and locked the door, the two men embraced. The bigger man pulled Foreman close, and when my target tilted his face upward, the bigger man covered his mouth with his own. The kiss was long and deep, and when it ended, Foreman said, "I've missed you, Domenico."

I should have packed it in right then. My plan had been to

take out my target late in the evening so that I would be far away
before anyone discovered his body the following day. I had not
planned for, did not desire and had been specifically instructed
to avoid collateral damage. I removed my index finger from the
trigger and rested it on the trigger guard, but I did not remove
my eye from the scope.

Foreman splashed three fingers of Jack Daniel's into a
tumbler and handed it to the big man, who knocked it back
in one long swallow. He wiped his mouth with the back of his
hand, a mannerism more consistent with a man of lower-class
upbringing than his smartly tailored suit implied. Money had
clearly not bought him class.

"Another?"

Domenico shook his head.

They spoke for a moment before Foreman untied the sash
and let his terry-cloth robe fall open. When Domenico saw the
sparkling blue jockstrap, a smile bisected his face. Then he loosened his tie, unthreaded it from his collar and dropped it over
the back of the black leather couch. He peeled off his jacket and
it joined the tie.

Foreman stepped forward to unbutton the big man's shirt,
starting at the neck, and he didn't stop when he reached the
bottom button. He unfastened Domenico's belt, unbuttoned his
trousers and tugged down his zipper. He dropped to his knees,
hesitated and looked up. He said something and Domenico
responded with a nod. Then Foreman reached into Domenico's
trousers and pulled out a thick, semierect cock that was rapidly
rising to its full potential. He wrapped one hand around the
stiffening shaft and took the swollen purple mushroom cap into
his mouth.

How I earn my living is much more than a job; it is also unex-
pectedly arousing. My cock was already erect from the thought

of what I'd been about to do, and it throbbed as I watched one man going down on another. I had seen many things through my riflescope while I was on the job, but I had never seen anything like this. I swallowed hard and kept watching.

Foreman took the entire length of Domenico's cock into his mouth and then pulled back. He did it again and again until the bigger man's cock glistened with saliva. By then Domenico had grown impatient with Foreman's slow oral caresses. He grabbed the back of Foreman's head, wrapped his thick, sausagelike fingers in Foreman's blond hair and held tight as he face-fucked the younger man.

Domenico suddenly stopped, the twisted expression on his face making it clear that he'd just erupted in Foreman's mouth. My target's Adam's apple bobbed up and down several times as he sought to swallow the load ejected against the back of his throat, but it was clear that he wasn't swallowing fast enough because a thin trickle of cum escaped from the corner of his mouth, slid down his chin and dripped to the carpet below.

Despite the cool evening breeze coming off the lake, my head was sweltering inside my watch cap. I used my left hand to wipe the sweat from my forehead, unzip my leather jacket and adjust the bulge in the crotch of my Levi's. I had traveled halfway around the world from my island home to eliminate a man with extreme prejudice, and I couldn't complete the contract because he was entertaining a guest. I knew I should abort the assignment before a civilian spotted me kneeling on the roof and wondered why I was dressed entirely in black and had a high-powered rifle pointed down the block, but still I kept watching.

After Domenico helped Foreman to his feet, my target shrugged the white terry-cloth robe from his shoulders and let it slide down his arms to pool on the carpet at his feet. Domenico smiled and slapped one cheek of Foreman's ass with the flat of his hand. Then he slapped the other cheek, leaving a red hand-print each time. Foreman laughed and said, "Think you'll be able to do it again?"

I couldn't see Domenico's lips to know his reply, but I tracked the two men as Domenico chased my target from the living room to the bedroom, where Foreman flopped on the pastel-blue comforter and lay on his back watching Domenico. The bigger man sat heavily on the side of the bed, unlaced and removed his black Oxfords, then peeled off his black socks and tucked them into his shoes. He stood, stripped off his trousers and hung them over the back of a chair. His white dress shirt, V-neck undershirt, and baggy white BVDs followed. The heavy salt at his temples extended southward to the hair on his barrel chest, his thick but firm abdomen and the dense mat of his pubic hair. His thick, rapidly inflating phallus and heavy ball sac slapped his muscular thighs as he crossed the room and grabbed Foreman's ankle.

Domenico dragged the smaller man off the comforter and then spun Foreman around and bent him over the far side of the bed. With Domenico behind Foreman, I could watch both of their faces through my scope. The bigger man grabbed a tube of lube from the nightstand and squeezed a healthy dollop into Foreman's asscrack. Then he massaged it in with his thick paw until he was able to slide one lubed finger into Foreman's sphincter. He pistoned his finger in and out of Foreman several times before replacing it with his cock. He positioned himself behind my target and pressed his cockhead against the smaller man's asshole. Then he grabbed Foreman's slim hips and held tight as he slammed forward and drove his thick cock deep into Foreman's shit chute.

Foreman's eyes widened and he bit his bottom lip as Domenico drew back and pushed forward. I could only imagine the sound of Domenico's heavy balls slapping against Foreman as he pounded into the smaller man and the mewling sounds Foreman made with each of Domenico's powerful thrusts.

By then my throbbing cock was hard enough to pound nails, and I had to do something to relieve the pressure. I wanted to free myself from the confines of my clothes but I knew better. If I came on the brick parapet or the tar-paper roof, I would leave behind DNA evidence that would tie me to the scene more than any random fibers from my clothing.

I loosened my belt and removed my glove, then I slid my left hand under the waistband of my boxers. Wishing I had lotion or lube to smooth my dry, chapped hand, I grabbed my cock and, though it was difficult to keep the rifle still while I stroked myself, continued to watch Domenico slam into my target's ass. Before long, my hand's rhythm matched the rhythm of Domenico's hips.

Domenico came first, throwing back his head and letting loose some sort of primal scream as he slammed into Foreman one last time and held the smaller man's hips in a vise grip that was certain to leave bruises.

Several strokes later, I came in my shorts, hot sticky cum covering my fist as quickly as my cock spat it out. My eyelids fluttered and the rifle wavered until the orgasm passed. I pulled my hand from my boxers and wiped it on my thigh, leaving much of the viscous fluid on the leg of my Levi's before I wedged my hand back in my glove.

I had lost track of what was happening in the apartment. I pressed my eye to the riflescope again and refocused on the bedroom four blocks away. Domenico was flat on his back on the bed, apparently asleep. Foreman was beside him. He had slipped out of the jockstrap, revealing a cock that easily rivaled Domenico's for length, but not for thickness. He squeezed a drop of lube into his palm and began stroking himself while staring at the sleeping bulk of his partner.

I knew I couldn't eliminate my target that night, so I let him play with himself while I broke down the rifle and returned it to the foam-padded briefcase in which I transported it. Though I had not touched anything on the roof, fibers from my clothing might have clung to the tar paper under my knees or the brick parapet I'd leaned against, but I couldn't do anything about that except burn my clothes at the first opportunity.

I policed the area as best I could, grabbed my briefcase with my dismantled rifle securely packed inside and walked to a stairwell door I'd left unlocked. I hurried down several flights of stairs and exited the building through a side door.

As I walked to my car two blocks away, I used a disposable cell phone to dial a memorized number. When a woman answered, I said, "I was unable to complete the contract. He had company."

"I know," she said. "My husband."

From that one comment, I realized my client was not a professional. I smashed the phone and threw the parts in a Dumpster. I would complete the contract later. Right then I had a hard-on, knew where to find a discreet gay bar and had the rest of the night to kill.

DONKEY DUDE

Martin Delacroix

I'm a skulker: I spy on men when they're jerking off.

Watching a hot-looking guy stroke himself when he doesn't know you're observing is incredibly sexy. The poor devil thinks he's in a private situation, believes no one knows what he's up to. But *I* know. I see everything.

I love watching a guy's face contort when he reaches orgasm. His cock throbs and his cum spurts and it glistens on his belly like so many gemstones. It is *oh,* so sexy and—

What?

Have I ever been caught?

Umm...yeah.

I'll tell you what happened, if you'd like. But don't repeat the story to anyone, understand?

Okay, listen:

A few years ago a guy lived in my neighborhood; I didn't know his name. I called him Donkey Dude 'cause his dick was so large. He was close to my age at the time—early twenties—

and he must have been attending college because the desk in his bedroom was often stacked with books. He was always using his laptop computer, too. At night he'd study with a pencil stuck sideways in his mouth, and occasionally he'd write in a spiral notebook. Most nights he wore nothing but a pair of boxer shorts and his ball cap turned backward.

This guy's body was hot: shoulder muscles like shot puts, carved chest, flat belly, sinewy legs. And he was handsome, too: dark hair and eyes, cleft chin, dark stubble on his cheeks.

Donkey Dude was a creature of habit. Every weeknight around eleven he'd lock his door, then strip off his boxers and sit before his computer, looking at porn, what kind I couldn't see. He'd tease his dick with his fingers and play with his low-hanger nuts and very quickly his cock would stiffen. He kept a bottle of lube in his desk drawer and he'd grease himself up, then stroke. If the windows were open I could hear the lube smacking. Sometimes he would raise his knees and rest his feet on the seat of his chair. He'd squeeze a dollop of lube onto his middle finger and stick it up his butt; all the way, no joke.

I probably spied on Donkey Dude two or three times a week.

Then one Saturday I was buying beer at a package store in my neighborhood, and Donkey Dude came cruising in, dressed in a sweaty T-shirt, basketball shorts and sneakers. Of course he wore his ball cap backward. He was with two other guys dressed similarly, and all three looked and sounded the same: well over six feet, lean and muscular, with stubble on their faces, deep voices and knockout smiles. One of them, a blond guy with a turned-up nose, walked past me in the aisle, and I almost fainted when his hip brushed against my ass.

His skin smelled like wet oak leaves.

The three of them bought two cases of beer, a bottle of rum and a twelve-pack of cola. The guy behind the counter checked their IDs to be sure each was twenty-one, then he asked if they were having a party.

Oak Leaves said, "If you call three guys getting trashed a 'party,' then...*yeah.*"

Everyone laughed, then the trio left with their purchases.

That night, around ten, I arrived at Donkey Dude's home, a single-story, cinder-block structure with a two-car garage and a privacy fence in back. The fence was no problem. I climbed atop a trash can and hopped over. On this particular night Donkey Dude's bedroom was dark, and at first I thought, *Shit, they're partying someplace else.* But then I heard loud music and masculine laughter. The noise intensified in volume as I rounded the corner of the house. Peering through an awning-style window, I saw Donkey Dude and his two buddies standing in a room with a vaulted ceiling where a sound system blared rap music. A porno film played on a flat-screen TV. In the movie, a chick with huge tits sucked a guy's cock while, at the same time, another guy screwed her from the rear. Donkey Dude's coffee table was littered with beer cans.

Donkey Dude's friend, Oak Leaves, took a hit off a joint, then he passed it to the third guy, a fair-skinned, auburn-haired dude with major cheekbones and biceps like two softballs. A thick cloud of smoke hung in the room, and I smelled the burning weed. All three guys were shirtless, wearing just their basketball shorts and sneakers, and I grew stiff looking at their lean and muscled bodies.

Oak Leaves blew a stream of smoke, then he said to Donkey Dude, "Your folks should leave town more often."

Donkey Dude chuckled. Turning toward the auburn-haired guy, he said, "Bitch, give me a shotgun."

Bitch placed the joint between his lips, lit end inside his mouth. He stepped to Donkey Dude and their faces came together. Donkey Dude made a circle with his lips, then Bitch blew a jet of smoke into Donkey Dude's mouth.

My cock got stiff as a broom handle as I watched them. Pulling it out, I spit in my palm and stroked myself, staring at Donkey Dude and his carved chest. They passed the joint another time, then Donkey Dude stubbed it out in an ashtray. He whispered something to Oak Leaves, then to Bitch. Both guys nodded, then they left Donkey Dude alone in the room, and I presumed the two were fetching more beer.

Donkey Dude gave his attention to the flat-screen TV. Slipping his hand inside his basketball shorts, he toyed with his cock, and I thought, *Holy shit, he's going to whack off while they're gone.*

My balls moved in their sac and sweat broke out on my forehead. I pumped my fist, thinking, *Come on, Donkey, pull your shorts down and let me see your—*

Behind me a twig snapped and I froze.

What the...?

I swung my gaze just in time to see Oak Leaves lunge at me, his arms outstretched. Bitch was right behind him. I tried dodging Oak Leaves but he was quicker than me and he tackled me like an expert, driving me to the ground so hard he knocked the breath out of me.

He said, "Gotcha, faggot."

I'm five-seven, one hundred thirty-five pounds, so I didn't stand a chance against Oak Leaves. He lay on top of me while I tried catching my breath. I asked myself, *What will happen next? Will they beat me up or call the cops? And how did they know I was here in the first place?*

The two forced me to my feet, each gripping one of my arms, then they hustled me into the house, my cock bobbing before me. We passed through an empty garage, then a kitchen and into the room with the TV, where Donkey Dude sipped from a beer can. When he saw me his lips parted into a grin.

"Hey, pervert," he said in a mocking tone that made me shiver. "Enjoying the show?"

Bitch asked Donkey Dude, "Is this the punk you told us about?"

Donkey Dude nodded. "The one and only."

I dropped my gaze and worked my jaw from side to side. *Shit*, I thought, *he knew I was out there.*

Bitch flicked my cock with a finger. "Cute pecker," he said, and they all laughed.

I felt like crying.

Donkey Dude approached; he got his face in mine, and I smelled his beer breath. Up close his eyes had a piercing quality. His eyebrows were thick, his lashes long like a girl's.

Stroking my temple with a knuckle, he said, "You're shaking. Are you scared?"

I dropped my gaze and nodded.

"What's your name?"

I lied and told him I was Greg.

"Do you like me, Greg?"

I kept my gaze lowered, my mouth shut. To either side of me, Bitch and Oak Leaves snickered. Donkey Dude chucked my chin till I raised it and looked into his eyes. He said, "Are you a good cocksucker?"

Heat rose in my cheeks. Again, I lowered my gaze. What should I say?

Donkey Dude slapped my face so hard I saw spots before my eyes. My cheek felt like he'd stuck needles into it.

"Answer me, punk."

I thought, *Go ahead, say it...*

"Yes, I'm a good cocksucker."

Donkey Dude stroked my burning cheek with a fingertip. "That's better."

Bitch asked Donkey Dude, "What should we do? Kick the crap out of him?"

Donkey Dude patted his chin. "I've got a better idea: let's get this punk naked and have ourselves some fun."

Bitch and Oak Leaves hooted. They shoved me to the carpet and tore at my clothing, and quite soon I was bare-assed and writhing on the floor, my face aflame. Donkey Dude left the room for a long moment then returned with a riding crop and pair of chrome handcuffs.

"Where'd you get those?" Oak Leaves asked.

Donkey Dude handed Oak Leaves the riding crop. "Remember Crystal? The blond chick I dated?"

"Sure."

Donkey Dude grinned. "She liked her kink."

They all laughed while Donkey Dude secured my hands behind my back; then they got me on my knees, turned so I faced away from the television.

My thoughts raced. What would they do with me?

Despite my fear, my cock remained stiff as PVC pipe.

Donkey Dude looked at his friends. "Who wants the first blow job?"

Bitch said to Donkey Dude, "He's your boyfriend; you go first."

Donkey Dude positioned himself so his crotch was right in my face. I guess they hadn't showered after their basketball game, and already I smelled his groin sweat. He pointed to a spot behind me and to my left, then he told Oak Leaves, "Stand there and use that crop on his ass if he's not doing his best. Got it?" Oak Leaves giggled and took his position. I heard him tap the crop against his palm.

Donkey Dude shucked his shorts and boxers. His monster cock and walnut-sized balls exploded into view, the former already stiff and twitching. The glans was plum shaped and violet in color, the shaft as smooth and white as cream cheese. He'd shaved his sac and trimmed his dark pubic bush, accentuating the size of his cock.

Clutching a fistful of hair on the back of my head, he forced me to look up into his face. In the same mocking voice he'd used earlier, he said, "Ready to suck cock, faggot?" Then he rubbed his erection against my cheek, the one he'd earlier slapped.

I was so scared I couldn't speak.

Donkey Dude looked at Oak Leaves. "Give him a couple of licks. Then maybe he'll answer."

The crop whistled through the air, then it connected with my asscheeks, making a sound like a pistol shot. I felt a band of fire across my backside and I cried out, just as Oak Leaves struck a second blow, drawing a howl from me. I mean, that crop *hurt*.

Donkey Dude yanked my hair again, so I was forced to look at him.

"I asked you a question, Greg. Are you going to suck my cock like a good faggot?"

I bobbed my chin and babbled like an idiot. I said, "I'll do whatever you want."

Donkey Dude grinned, then he nudged my lips with the head of his cock. "Open up, punk."

When I did he drove into me, his glans poking the back of my throat and making me gag. Christ, he was big. My nose was buried in his pubic bush and, again, I smelled his groin sweat. He rocked his hips, hands resting on the crown of my head, while I applied pressure to the shaft of his cock, using my tongue and lips. When I looked up at Donkey Dude his gaze was fixed on the TV. He licked his lips while his cock plunged in and out of my throat.

After a minute or so, he slapped the side of my head.

"You're lazy," he told me. Then he told Oak Leaves. "Whack his ass."

The crop sizzled my behind—once, twice, three times—while I squealed.

Jesus *Christ*, it hurt.

I redoubled my efforts, picking up the pace, and very soon Donkey Dude's breath huffed. He grabbed the back of my head and pulled my nose back into his pubic hair, and I felt his cock throb against my tongue. His hips jerked a time or two, then he unloaded several shots of sour-tasting semen. I didn't want another lick from the crop, so I swallowed every bit of Donkey Dude's load, knowing he expected nothing less.

Things, of course, did not end there.

Oh, no.

When Donkey Dude's breathing slowed and his cock slid from my mouth, he patted my head like I was a house pet. He asked his friends, "Who's next?"

I looked up at Bitch and Oak Leaves, thinking, *What now?*

Oak Leaves pointed at the flat-screen TV; he said to Bitch, "See what they're doing to that chick?"

Bitch nodded.

Oak Leaves said, "Let's try it. I'll fuck his ass while he sucks you off."

I trembled while they positioned me on the carpet, on my knees and elbows. Both Oak Leaves and Bitch got naked. Oak Leaves's cock was nearly as big as Donkey Dude's. His groin area was shaved smooth as a twelve-year-old's. Bitch had a long, slender cock and an ass like two cantaloupes. Both guys smelled funky, unwashed as they were.

Donkey Dude handed Oak Leaves a condom, and I watched

Oak Leaves roll it down the shaft of his cock. At the time I'd only been fucked a few times in my life, and the thought of taking Oak Leaves's cannon up my chute scared the crap out of me.

Bitch knelt before me. He tapped my cheek with his cock and I lowered my jaw, then he slid inside me, the rancid smell of his groin making me wince.

"That feels g-o-o-d," Bitch said.

Behind me, Oak Leaves knelt and his knees cracked. Patting my stinging behind, he said, "Ready, fag?"

When I didn't answer he slapped my asscheek—hard—and I cried out.

"Answer me or I'll use the crop again."

Spitting out Bitch's cock, I cried, "Yes, Sir. Please, fuck me."

Everyone but me laughed.

"That's better," Oak Leaves said. Spreading my buttcheeks, he whistled while he stroked my pucker with a fingertip. "Cute little hole, Greg."

When Oak Leaves entered me I felt as though he were tearing me apart. I squealed, deep in my throat, while my mouth worked Bitch's cock. My pucker went into spasms, flexing against the shaft of Oak Leaves's cock. I sucked air through my nose while tears leaked from the corners of my eyes. I wanted to spit out Bitch's cock and beg Oak Leaves to withdraw, to relieve the burning in my anus, but I knew my plea would fall on deaf ears.

They owned my ass.

I sucked Bitch's cock as best I could, and I guess he enjoyed it 'cause he kept on saying, "Yeah, just like that. You're a sweet little faggot."

Behind me, Oak Leaves thrust his hips. His pelvis slapped my punished bottom while his cock stretched my pucker and poked my prostate, and very soon I felt warmth in my limbs and chest, each time he plunged into me. I'd forgotten how good it felt to have my ass stuffed with cock: already my balls tingled and my cock dripped.

Bitch came first, filling my mouth with his briny-tasting jizz. He moaned as he shot, his body jerking with every spurt. He stayed inside my mouth and toyed with my ears while I swallowed and Oak Leaves kept thrusting. Oak did this another five minutes before his cock throbbed within me. He shouted like a crazy man when he came, one hand resting on my sweaty back while his semen jetted inside me.

Then, the coolest thing happened:

While Oak Leaves gasped for air, Donkey Dude knelt beside me. He reached for my cock and worked my foreskin a few times and, right away, I lost it. I moaned, then my body jerked and I shot a load all over the carpet, several healthy spurts.

Donkey Dude chuckled, still holding my cock in his fingers. "I think the faggot likes us."

My cheeks burned while my lungs heaved. Even after Bitch and Oak Leaves withdrew, I remained on my knees and elbows, breath huffing, my hair damp with sweat. All I could think was, *Holy shit that was sexy.*

They took the handcuffs off, but they kept me naked in the house a few hours before letting me go. For a time I sat on Donkey Dude's lap like I was a little boy. He played with my cock while we all drank rum and colas. The three of them talked about their basketball game, school and girls, and they even asked me a few questions about myself. A couple of times Donkey Dude mussed my hair. He told me I was a fine cocksucker, and Bitch said he had to agree. I gave a fine blow job, he said.

"Your ass is sweet, too," Oak Leaves told me. "Better than pussy."

Donkey Dude took me to the home's master bath. He got

naked and we climbed into the shower and scrubbed each other
with soap and a washcloth.

While we stood under the nozzle I said to Donkey Dude,
"Tell me something."

"What?"

"How long have you known I've been watching you?"

Shrugging, he said, "A few months, maybe."

"Why didn't you stop me? You could've closed the drapes or
something."

Donkey Dude looked at me and grinned.

"Why spoil the fun?" he said.

You never know what may happen when you roam the alleys
and peep. It could lead to something better, something unbeliev-
ably sexy. Think about it; you might like skulking as much as I
do.

Have I seen those guys again?

Well, *yeah*. I wouldn't say we are close friends or anything.
But Donkey Dude (real name Travis) has my cell phone number
and once a month or so, when his folks are not home, he'll call
me and I'll come over. Sometimes it's just him, sometimes the
other guys are there, but it's always hot.

When it's just me and Travis, he'll often stand naked at his
bedroom window, stroking himself while I jerk outside in the
bushes.

"I like it when you watch me," he said once. "I know you
like it too."

"Oh, yeah," I told him. "That's a fact, Donkey Dude."

SHAFTED

Harley Jackson

The place was a shithole, and that's the best I can say about it. When they said I was going to San Francisco on a week's contract gig, I was excited. I'd always wanted to go, and this was a chance to do it on the company nickel. Consulting in the daytime, and I'd have evenings to myself. "A nice hotel downtown," they said, but I should have known right then. When was the last time you ever heard of a nice hotel called the *Savoy?*

The cheap bastards didn't even get me a room overlooking the street. Not that Ellis Street is in any way picturesque, but there was a heat wave on and no air-conditioning. Instead, my window looked into a fetid air shaft. Seven other grimy windows completed the octagon-shaped hole, which extended three stories above mine and one below. And behind each window was a grotty little room, just like mine, with a guy in his underwear sitting on the bed, except for one room that was all but packed, floor to ceiling, with newspapers. I could barely see the guy in the narrow passage he had left open.

"That's Delacruz," a voice said beside me. "He's our resident librarian." I looked at the window to my immediate right and saw a burly bald guy in a tank top leaning on the sill. "There's one in every hotel, you know."

"One what?" I replied, curious to hear the diagnosis.

"Newspaper hoarder. Every hotel's got at least one. Name's Deblonski. Call me Blondie."

"I'm Ross. Nice place you got here."

He sniffed. "It's a shithole."

Well, we were in agreement on that. The tiny room was as depressing as its view and stuffy as hell, so I went out for a walk around the area. I'd be willing to bet you could find a more run-down neighborhood, but it would take a search. I had heard of Castro Street, Polk Street and South of Market, and I had hoped to visit the clubs and bars they were famous for, but this place didn't seem to be near any of them. I wandered until it got dark, then went back to the hotel. At least it would be more bearable in the evening air.

The shaft was different at night. All the windows were lit from the inside, throwing a sick yellow light into the open space. Each inhabitant on my floor was clearly visible inside his cell. Delacruz hunched over a newspaper, his long slim finger scanning each line as he read. Blondie smoked, leaning on the windowsill. As my light was off, he didn't see me. A shirtless young tough to my left paced back and forth. A nearly naked fat man listened to the radio. Nobody seemed to have a television. A wiry old man lay in bed reading a book. A bewildered-looking fellow sat in his chair by the window, glancing around in different directions. An average man of middle age was doing absolutely nothing. *Inmates of the asylum,* I thought. *Well, fuck it.* I peeled down to T-shirt and boxers, turned on the light and pulled my chair up to the window.

"Hi, neighbor," said Blondie.

"Hey."

"Get tired of walking?"

"Yeah, I guess so. Say, where are all the bars around here?"

"Polk Street. You gay?"

"Yeah, why?"

"You wanna turn right. Walk down four blocks and turn right. That's where most of the gay bars are."

"Thanks. Quiet here tonight, huh?"

Blondie gave an amused snort. "It's usually pretty quiet here. Sometimes things get exciting. It's still early."

We chatted awhile and passed his pint of Yukon Jack, until I decided to work on my presentation. I sat on the bed and pulled the chair over to use as a table. Voices rose and fell in the shaft outside. I paid no attention. I reviewed my notes until I saw something move outside the window. A dark-skinned man in boxer shorts was climbing down the drainpipe. He smiled as he went by. "Don't mind me, bro. Just getting some cool air, you know?"

I smiled back. He was handsome, about my age. "Where do you find cool air in this joint?" I replied.

"Come on down."

I went to the window. The guy was lying on a towel at the bottom of the shaft.

"He says it's cooler down there," Blondie explained. "I never went down to find out."

"Blondie's too fat to get through the window," the guy said, and laughs echoed around the shaft.

Blondie laughed too. "Hey, if I was so inclined—well, you get the idea anyway."

"Yeah, I'll bet you jack off on me again tonight. Don't tell me about your inclinations." More laughter.

"Aw, hell, I just had to piss, that's all, and my sink was stopped up." That really broke it up. Heads began to poke out of their windows.

"Naw, come on down, Ross, it's cool. We're a pretty happy family around here. None of these nasty motherfuckers is gonna piss on us, right, guys?"

"Not unless you pay me," someone high above yelled, and the laughter broke loose again.

"Hey," Blondie said, "you were looking for excitement, right?" He threw me a wink.

Everyone was looking, even Delacruz. I felt a little awkward, but knew it would be worse to chicken out and go to bed. "Yeah, fuck it," I said, and threw my towel out the window. Hushed voices murmured in the shaft. I opened the window wide and swung my legs over the sill. The pipe was easy to climb down.

He had spread my towel next to his on the floor of the shaft. I hopped down and immediately felt the cool air. "See what I mean? We're right above the restaurant's freezer. Hi, I'm Vince." He stuck out his hand and I felt his strong grip. "What union are you?"

"Pardon?"

"Aren't you with one of the sailor's unions?"

"No, I'm a computer geek."

"No shit? Most of us here are sailors. Figured you might be SUP, that's my union. Most of these guys are SIU, but there's some IBU trash here too."

"Fuck you, Vince," said a good-natured voice high above.

"Anyway," Vince continued, "you got a sailor's build: nice upper body strength."

"Thanks," I said, and lay back on the towel. The surface was hard, but it was a fair trade escaping the heat. Above me, the shaft glowed yellow, and silhouetted dark faces peeked out of windows. The lowest level of windows was just a few feet above us. Eight faces watched us intently. Up and down the shaft, cigarette cherries flared and glowed. "I see what you mean about a happy family," I said.

"Yeah, it ain't bad. Place is a shithole, but it's ours."

In the dim light, I saw that Vince had his cock out and was stroking it lazily. He was long rather than wide, and circumcised. He noticed me looking. "You like it, Ross? Why don't you get some air yourself?"

"Don't mind if I do," I said, peeling off my T-shirt and balling it up for a pillow. I took my cock out and matched Vince's easy pace. Chatter in the shaft dropped to whispers. We had everyone's attention. I could pick out Blondie's round head next to my empty window. He waved.

"You know," Vince whispered, "there're two kinds of people in the world: people who make things happen and people who watch things happen. You're the first one ever come down here with me like this. I'd say you're like me. You make things happen. These clowns," he indicated the faces at the windows with a wave, "they just watch. But it's cool, 'cause deep down they wish they were us." He shifted around so that we were lying head to foot, his cock just inches from my face. "You want to trade off for a while?"

I resumed stroking where he had left off. His meat was half-hard and hot to the touch. I could feel his pulse beating in it. His rough hand closed around my cock and worked me up and down. The chafing of his calluses was a nice change from my own baby-soft palm, and from the hands of the white-collar guys I usually dated. We stroked each other for a while, neither of us in any hurry. Occasional moans from above told of spectators getting in on the action. It just made it hotter.

Finally, Vince rolled onto his side and took my cock in his

mouth. His bone prodded me in the cheek, and I sucked it into
my mouth. He was still flexible, and I had no trouble getting him
deep into my throat. His wiry pubes brushed my lips.

"Damn, you're good!" he said out loud. "Shit, Ross, that's
fucking incredible." He went back to sucking me, one hand
stroking my shaft while the other tugged at my balls. I felt warm
wet droplets hit my skin. "Aw, man," Vince hollered, "who was
that?" Laughter rang out. "Fucking night is still young, and now
you're on the sidelines."

I was really warming up to Vince. He wasn't anything like
the guys I was used to. I made a mental note to check out some
sailor bars while I was in town. Vince seemed to be enjoying me
too. As he grinned in the dim light, I moved over and kissed him.
He met me head on, opening his mouth and sucking my tongue
in. He clamped his arms around me and gripped me tight. Above
us, the chatter changed tone. Our every move created a reaction from the gallery above. I put my hands in his hair, and the
tone changed again. I got the feeling they were less interested
in kissing. They wanted us to get on with the sex. Vince was
reading the reaction the same as I was.

"Don't pay no attention, it's just some of these guys aren't
really gay. They like jacking off, but kissing makes them
uneasy."

A voice close by said, "I like it. You guys are totally hot."

"Well, come on down and join the fun," Vince replied.

"No, thanks, I just like to watch."

"Just like I said," Vince whispered in my ear. "Hey!" he called
out above, "anybody got a rubber?" Several landed around us,
but the guy right above me leaned out to hand me one. I took it
from his outstretched fingers and saw him give me a thumbs-up.

"Thanks," I said.

"Thank *you*," he replied.

"See what I mean?" Vince called out. "There's nothing like an appreciative audience. They'll be throwing tens and twenties before we're done." That got a big laugh. "Yeah, 'cause you're all a bunch of broke motherfuckers!" He turned back to me. "So how do you like it, Ross? Me, I go either way, so I'll give you the honors."

I smiled and handed him the rubber. "Don't be afraid to be rough," I offered.

"Oh, you like it navy style, huh? Yeah, I was in the navy. Them boatswain's mates all like it rough." He got to his knees and rolled the rubber onto his cock. I lay back and raised my ass. His muscular hands gripped my butt and he fingered my hole. We were so wet with sweat that he slid inside easily, first one finger, then two. I relaxed and let him take charge. He hiked me up and plunged inside in a single thrust. A collective murmur of approval sounded from above. Vince leaned back and drove upward into me, pulling my ass close with each thrust. His wet thighs slapped against me. He was ramming me all the way down with every stroke. It was the best dicking I'd had in a long time, and the fact that forty guys had their eyes glued on us made it that much hotter. He let out a long groan. "Hey, Ross, you might want to turn over at some point," he managed to say. "You don't want no cum hitting you in the eyes—you could go blind, you know?"

From personal experience I knew better. "No fucking way," I breathed. "I want to be able to see."

"You like an audience, huh? Yeah, me too." He lifted my legs onto his shoulders, and suddenly he was thrusting even deeper. God, he was long. I felt his hand grip my cock, stroking me in time with his thrusts. A loud moan echoed up above us. Someone was coming. I saw one of the silhouettes hunch over, then buck upright again. He leaned out, holding the windowsill, and drained his cock over us. Hot drops landed on my bicep. The smell of semen filled the airshaft. *What a fucking sewer,* I thought. *Goddamn hole in a building with me lying in the bottom of it, getting fucked by a sailor while a bunch of horny bastards jerk off over us.* It was the hottest sex I'd ever had. Somebody else came, and it started a chain reaction, the grunts and snorts all blending together as Vince slammed my ass and worked my cock. I couldn't hold out much longer. Vince couldn't either, judging by the way he was moving. His rhythm picked up, but his steadiness was gone. He was bucking against my ass like a bronco. Then he let me have it. "Aw, yeah!" he yelled and rammed me to the hilt. I felt his body jerking with spasms. That sent me over the edge. I blew my load all over my chest. Jizz dribbled down his knuckles and onto my belly. Another shot hit me in the shoulder. It wasn't mine. Up the shaft, they were still rocking, but definitely on the downhill side. Vince let my legs down and eased himself on top of me. His moans gradually turned into sounds of satisfaction.

"Hey, how long are you planning on staying?" he asked, while we caught our breaths.

"Week..." was all I had the wind to say.

"I know a club that has a steam room," he offered. "Of course, they don't have these charming bastards," he laughed, "but they have some good arenas for social fucking. You really like an audience, am I right?"

I just lay back and laughed. I had never really thought about it before, but he was right. I doubted that private sex would ever again be as hot for me as this.

HOT, BUTTERED BONER

Rob Rosen

had one of those weird work schedules: off on Mondays and Tuesdays, toiling away on the weekends. It fucked with my social life but made for good moviegoing. I mean, it's not like anyone else went to the theater midday on a Tuesday, just me and the odd granny or two, the occasional night-shift worker, the unemployed, college kids. Meaning I pretty much had the place to myself half the time.

Which is why the dude stood out that day: tall and lean; scruffy; black hair, all wavy-like; olive complexion; large honker; emerald eyes; hairy knuckles. All of this I saw while on line for popcorn, my hand brushing his as I moved away, his green eyes locking on to my muddy brown ones for the briefest of seconds, a spark running down my spine like wildfire. I responded with a smile and a nod, felt a rumble in my pants.

With my knees slightly buckling, I made it back to my particular theater, taking a seat dead center; there was a smattering of other moviegoers here and there, all in different rows, staring ahead, watching, waiting—typical. Though what happened next was anything but.

The lights dimmed, the previews started and someone headed down my lonely row. Oddly, he sat right next to me, placing his super-sized popcorn bag on the floor and removing his jacket. "I sit here, yes?" came the voice, deep, with a thick accent, elongated vowels, truncated syllables.

I stared up at green eyes dappling in the screen light, a smile stretched wide on his handsome face. "Um, sure," I managed, my heart suddenly racing.

He sat, jacket over his lap, popcorn lifted up, face forward. The preview was loud and frenetic. Still, I could hear my neighbor getting up to something, butt shifting, arms moving back and forth, his leg suddenly pressed up next to mine, his jacket placed on the seat next to him before he settled down, popping handfuls of the buttery snack in his mouth, chomping happily away.

The movie started soon thereafter. His leg was still pressed up tightly against mine, mine pushing back, his arm on the rest, mine next to his; his hand was suddenly in my hand, giving a friendly squeeze, and my breath grew ragged. "Is okay, yes?" he asked.

"Um, yes," I exhaled, my mind reeling, my hand sweaty but holding steady. Fucking weird, but who was I to argue?

Ten minutes into the movie and, naturally, I hadn't a clue what was happening on the screen. All I could think about was his hand, his knee, the popcorn moving up and disappearing from my line of sight. "You want?" he asked, in between eager mouthfuls.

"I have my own," I replied. "But thanks."

"No, is okay. You take," he insisted, shaking the bag in his lap.

So I let go of his hand and reached in, my hand brushing

popcorn and then something else; something thick, hard, pulsing. Fuckin' A, the dude had stuck his woody through the bottom of the bag—sick mind, but genius, just the same. I gave it a squeeze, and his moan rumbled through both our seats. "Cracker Jacks never had surprises like this," I whispered in his ear after leaning over; I delivered a lick to his lobe, a tender bite down.

He turned and whispered back, "No surprise. Is dick. Is okay? You look. I like you to look." We were now nose to nose, his breath warm on my face, the last word hotly drawn out.

I chuckled and stared down, my hand still in the bag, his dick firmly in my grip: beautiful, buttery slick, thick as a dozen Twizzlers. Twenty minutes later, the popcorn was gone, but his boner remained, seven steely inches of it. Seven steely inches I now ached to see, to taste, to get the fuck out of that paper bag. "Mind if we leave?" I asked, leg bouncing, an eddy of adrenaline swirling in my belly.

"Why, you no like movie?" he asked, a tremor to his raspy voice.

I rapid-stroked his cock, trying to the keep the bag-crinkling down to a minimum. "I haven't been able to follow it all that well."

He paused. "Okay. Wait." The jacket was lifted and put back over his lap. Five minutes later, the bag was gone and, sadly, so was his rigid prick. "We go now."

He stood and walked down the row and up the aisle. I followed close behind, my breathing suddenly shallow, cock ready to explode. We emerged into the hallway light, face-to-face, both of us nervous, unsure. Intimate strangers.

"Where would you like to go?" I asked, looking up coyly, his eyes drawing me in, swirling green against a sea of dark skin, his teeth pearly white, the smile big and wide and beguiling. He looked around, then turned back my way.

"I have idea. You like, um, little adventure?"

"Do I get to see that dick of yours outside of a paper bag?"

He nodded, winked.

"No more bag, promise. You follow. All will be okay." He looked down the hall again, I guessed to make sure the coast was clear. Then he grabbed my hand and pulled me in front of the bathroom. "You wait here. Be right back."

He disappeared inside. I scratched my head and waited, shifting nervously from one foot to the other. Thankfully, he came out a few seconds later, one of those yellow placards warning that the bathroom was closed for cleaning hanging from his hand. He quickly pulled me inside the john and then set the sign on the carpet outside.

We were alone again, surrounded by blue tile, three urinals, four stalls, three sinks.

"What if someone ignores the sign?" I asked as he yanked me up to him, chest to chest, his hands cupping my ass.

"Little adventure turn big, I think." He smiled and laughed, his full lips on mine, soft as down, like a perfect screen kiss, made even better when his mouth parted and a deft tongue snaked and coiled its way inside. My moan ricocheted around the room, our bodies meshed together. "My name is Stefan," he informed me in between hungry sucks and slurps, hands roaming north to south.

"Jeff," I whispered into his mouth. "Nice to meet you."

He pulled away and sat on the edge of the row of sinks. There was a pause, while he formulated his words.

"I go to movies to learn English."

"Seems like you learned a bit more than that," I chided.

"Ah, yes. Popcorn trick. Is fun, yes?"

"Inventive, at any rate. What else you got for me?" I winked and grabbed my tenting crotch.

He echoed the wink with one of his own, a finger held up high, a silent *Wait and see.* He set his jacket down on the counter, his hands unbuttoning the top button of his shirt, then another, revealing a thick matting of chest hair, a cleft between two chiseled pecs. Another button or two exposed a six-pack with some extra cans. One last button, the shirttails were pulled out, and the shirt dropped to the floor.

"You like, yes?" he whispered, devilishly sexy.

"I like, yes." I started to unbutton my own shirt, but he lifted his finger up, yet again.

"No, you wait. Watch me for now. Is better than movie, I think."

I shrugged and bade him continue, the plot, apparently, thickening. Well, that and my swelling cock. He nodded, kicked off his shoes, rolled down his socks, exposing big feet, with high arches and wiry hair running across the top. He saw me looking and lifted a foot up for closer inspection. I crouched down and held it in my hand, my tongue darting out for a zoom around his big toe, which was soon engulfed by my mouth, then each toe in kind, this little piggy going happily to market. He moaned with each slurp, the sound traveling down his body and out my own.

"You suck good," he grunted.

"You ain't seen nothing yet."

"*Ain't* is bad English," he informed me with a wry grin.

"Thanks, I'll make a note of it." I stood up and pointed midsection. "Pants, please."

He hopped off the counter and reached for the top button, *pop,* then the zipper, *zip.* The pants were pushed down, slowly, the scene drawn out, the crescendo yet to come. He peeled them off, wearing nothing but a pair of green boxers, tightly fitting around tree-trunk-thick thighs, fine black hairs circling around and around, working their way down.

"Hairy motherfucker," I rasped.

"Yes, very. You like?" He gave a lick of his lips, his hand tweaking a nipple, thick and pink, fully engorged.

"I like. A lot."

He smiled and turned around, his face to the mirror, staring at me in the reflection. "Good. Then Stefan has something even better for you."

His thumbs slipped inside the waistband, pushed down, and his crack was soon revealed, hair trailing down and spreading out. More crack, more hair, and my mouth was watering like Pavlov's dog. Boxers all the way down now, beautiful compact ass in full-moon mode, he leaned over, elbows on the counter. It had to be the hairiest ass this side of the Mississippi. The other side, too.

"*Better* doesn't begin to cover it," I groaned, locking eyes with him in the mirror.

He reached behind and spread his cheeks, hairy within, circling a pink, crinkled, winking hole. "Yes, very hairy. Soft like feather, though." He spread his feet farther apart, his massive balls hanging down, swaying. "Is good, yes?"

"Is good. Fuck, yes."

He laughed, the sound like pebbles washed along the shore, then turned back around, his thick tool springing into view, jutting straight out: dark meat, veined, plum-sized head dripping with precum, all topped with a thick, black bush. The dude was wall-to-wall carpet. He gave his prick a tug and a stroke, balls bouncing as he hopped on the counter again. "Your turn, Jeff. My turn to watch." He groaned, purred. "I like to watch, Jeff."

I nodded and got down to business, eager to transition to the next scene. In an instant, my clothes sat in a heap, my cock thick, rigid, pointing up and a bit over to the side, already slick, gripped in my hand.

"Very nice," he sighed. "You look good naked, Jeff. Big dick. Pale body, little hair. Not like me. All hairy, dark. Like yin and yang, I think is called."

"And speaking of yangs," I quipped, moving in now.

He lifted his legs up and apart, leaning back: cock, balls, a hole all mine for the taking. "Buffet-style," he offered.

I bent down, face to ass-level, his hole an inch away. I breathed in, deeply, the heady aroma of musk and sweat wafting up my nose. My tongue jutted out, ready for the first taste. Close. So fucking close. But no friggin' cigar.

The door creaked open. "Hey!" came the shout from a dude dressed all in black, young, barely in his twenties, tall and gangly. "You're not the janitor."

"What gave it away?" I asked, falling backward onto my ass, my heart pounding, stomach in knots all of a sudden, this unforeseen plot twist completely unwelcomed.

"I should call the cops," he managed, an edge to his voice now. Another twist. The day was just full of them.

"Or you could just watch," I tried.

"Yes," chimed in my rigid partner. "You watch. We play. Is better than movie."

Usher dude twisted the meager hairs that sprouted from his chin, pushing down with his free hand on the stiffy obviously growing in his work slacks.

"Really?" Deep inhale, long exhale.

Stefan chuckled and nodded. "Yes. You watch. Two conditions. One, you lock door behind you."

A set of keys were quickly produced and the door locked, his head whipping back around. "And two?" he asked, panting now, eyes moving back and forth between the two of us.

Again the chuckle as Stefan hopped down, billy club of a dick swaying. I watched as he pulled down three sheets of paper towels and pumped a glob of pink hand sanitizer onto them, then ran into a stall and came out with a silver rod, minus its accompanying toilet paper. "Two," he replied, walking over to our new friend. "You fuck yourself with this while you watch." He turned to me with a wink and a nod. "Adventure continues, huh, Jeff?"

The usher's eyes went from us to the rod, his hands trembling as he undid his shirt, kicking off his shoes. "Um, okay," he replied, barely in a whisper. The shirt came off. The guy was way thin, hairless, with tight muscles, tiny pink nipples and a washboard tummy. His pants next, down and on the floor, showing thin, long legs. White briefs were yanked off to reveal a massive cock, nine inches easy, balls like boulders; a neat, trimmed bush the only hairs in sight. He sat on the ground, back against the tile, grabbing his feet, lifting his legs apart, exhibiting the smoothest asshole I'd ever seen.

"Put it in for me. Please," he pled, eyes big.

We both got on the ground in front of him, legs crossed. I slicked up his tree limb of a prick, then his pink, puckered hole, with the hand soap. Stefan gently slid the silver rod in, the usher grunting and groaning all the while, eyes glazed over, lids fluttering as the tool got worked inside, his prick pulsing in my grip.

"Now you watch," Stefan purred, leaning in for a quick kiss on his waiting mouth.

"Better than a double feature," I added, also with a kiss and a final stroke.

Then we hopped up and back into position, Stefan on the counter, me crouching beneath him. I glanced over my shoulder first, at the usher now fucking his ass with the rod, slowly, evenly, a matching stroke on his prick, an eager look on his face, ready for the show.

That made two of us.

Not wasting time this go-round, I dove in, lapping at his ring, shoving my tongue inside, eliciting a grunt from him as he slapped his hefty prick on my forehead. My tongue traveled north, through a forest of hair, circling his nuts, one popping in my mouth, then the other, my finger tickling his hole all the while. Farther north I went, up, up, up, lapping at his still buttery, salty shaft, one finger now up his chute as my mouth went south, engulfing him in one fell swoop.

"Fucking hot," he grunted.

"Fucking hot," the usher echoed from across the room, eyes locked on our scene. I would've thirded the opinion, but my mouth was still busy, sucking and slurping on all that beautiful dark meat while he pumped it down my throat, his hands now on the back of my neck, pushing me into his crotch, his balls soon lapping up against my chin. He lifted his legs higher, legs farther apart, my index finger joined by both its neighbors, up and in and back, all the way, deep inside his ass; a long, steady exhale came from between his parted lips, while his cock pulsed in my mouth.

I retracted, popping his prick out, my mouth licking up his belly and lean, hairy torso, all slick with sweat, to take a nipple in my mouth for a suck and a bite as I finger-fucked his ass with one hand and stroked his dick with the other. Farther up I went, till we were mouth to mouth, our kiss hungry, insistent, his eyes open, reeling me in.

He moved his face slightly back.

"I know how to end this movie, Jeff," he whispered into my mouth. "Let's spunk on *him*." He tilted his head toward the usher.

"Perfect ending," I whispered back. "The audience will love it."

I slid my fingers out of his ass, Stefan hopped down and both of us headed over to where the usher's eyes were staring up. He gave a gulp, his Adam's apple rising and falling, smiled and nodded, shoving the rod all the way inside his ass, with a quickening stroke on his long prick. He knew what was coming next. Or who. Three voyeurs. Three exhibitionists. A perfect trio.

Stefan and I stood side by side, one of my hands working my cock, the other inside his ass. Stefan did the same, both of us in sync, our dicks pointed down, the usher's pointed up: big boners ready to explode.

And explode they did, a split second later, all at once, in a Vesuvius of cum.

Our legs quaked, our heads were thrown back, moans circling the room, assholes clenched tight as we shot and shot and shot, thick streams of cum that rained down on him. And then the usher came, too, his massive tool spewing, eyes still gazing at our shooting dicks, panting, groaning, his sweaty torso twitching as he worked every last drop out.

"I like this movie," Stefan rasped, trying to catch his breath.

"Two thumbs-up," I added.

"Three," amended the usher.

We helped him to his feet, the silver rod gliding out and quickly tossed, all three of us wiping off and getting dressed. The usher poked his head out of the restroom first, then looked back at us. "Ready for the sequel whenever you are," he offered, before leaving us alone again.

Stefan smiled and leaned in for a soft kiss, a pat on my ass. "Sequels are never as good as the original," he said. "We make new movie next time. Just you and me."

"And where will we be filming?" I asked, both of us heading out of the bathroom.

He laughed and handed me a card he'd taken from his wallet.

I looked down, smiled, looked back up. "You come. Three days from now, okay?"

"A new little adventure?" I asked.

"Oh, big one this time. Very big."

And that it was, the room full of people, a dozen dialects in my ears, happy faces on all in attendance, happier still from the group of fifty down in front. Stefan stood, back row, the biggest grin of all when he saw me enter.

"Ain't it beautiful?" he hollered, pointing to the flag, his flag now.

"*Ain't* is bad English," I hollered back.

"I'll make a note of it!" He bent over and then quickly reappeared, a giant bag of popcorn held up for me to see. I laughed and held up mine, great minds obviously thinking alike, a new plot twist already in the works. No cameo appearances this go-round, just the two stars of the movie, like Thelma and Louise, Butch and Sundance—Stefan and Jeff.

THE ROOKIE

Gregory L. Norris

So there you are on another hot and lazy summer afternoon indistinguishable from a line of brutal dog days, stripped down to your underwear, sitting in front of the TV. The air conditioner runs at full blast. You're flipping channels, not really interested or even alive as much as going through the motions. You'll eat a boring, predictable dinner; fall asleep on the sofa, in front of the tube. You'd jerk your dick if it didn't require so much effort—getting up, fishing through the same stack of banal studio DVDs, laboring to get excited watching a bunch of dudes with shaved chests and bored expressions go though choreographed, robotic sex. Or you could beat off to the baseball game, imagining all those athletic straight jocks with their firm butts, big feet and sweating nut sacs acting a little crazy with the ass-slapping and the frat-boy behavior in the locker room.

You could, but that would require you to use your imagination and that, too, has gone into hibernation. In fact, you think with a humorless chuckle, the brisk air pouring out of your house's two window units isn't just refrigerating the house but also your corpse, keeping it intact, keeping you from rotting. You're already dead on the inside, having lost the will to live, so the rest is inevitable, mere biology. You can't avoid it, so why try? Your headstone could read: *Here lies the body of a man who died too soon, because he stopped living too young.*

You even start writing your own obituary in your head, only that takes too much work, and your thoughts return to jacking on your dick, which sits half-swollen along the elastic waistband of your tighty-whities. You give it a few firm tugs, scratch at your balls, sniff your fingers in search of the pungent ripeness of a man's finest scent, only the smell that greets your nostrils is sweet, too fresh—fabric softener, from this particular pair of underwear's last trip through the dryer. There's formaldehyde flowing through your veins, not blood. Life as you used to know it is over.

You don't remember falling asleep, and it's not like you sleep anymore so much as drift into the night version of the day's fugue state. And it's not really night outside, but twilight. Seven o'clock and change, according to the clock on the cable box. The nights are coming quicker—next month, it'll be dark by six. Now, it's only gray out, a fitting color for your existence.

The sound that woke you up and sent your heart out of its sluggishness and into a gallop comes again. Hard yet elegant, it shakes the house and, at first, you mistake it for thunder. There wasn't a cloud in the sky last time you rolled your half-shut eyes toward a window, and no storms on the horizon, according to the weatherman. Then you hear the steady chug, realize the cadence is too precise to be another summer tempest; this storm is entirely man-made.

And, *oh, man,* what you see when you drag your carcass out

of the TV room and over to the kitchen windows on the side of the house that faces the rental property next door that's sat empty since the spring. It's one of those sport bikes, colored a fiery shade of red, the red of fresh blood; an expensive machine, no doubt; a real youthful, manly machine—what they call a crotch rocket: a bike with balls.

Balanced on its spine is a body that can only belong to a minor Greek deity, Phaeton perhaps, he who reportedly pulled the sun across the sky on that ill-fated flaming chariot ride millennia ago. How you remember this bit of high school minutia is beyond you; high school is twenty-seven years gone by. Maybe it's seeing what gets off that sport bike that shoots a jolt of electricity through your atrophied corpse, bringing you back to life like Mary Shelley's stitched-together collection of spare body parts.

The rider, the god, wears a T-shirt, damp between the shoulders. Because of his stance on the bike, it rides up his back, exposing the waistband and a length of black boxer-brief. Shorts, military cutoffs by the look of them, showcase hairy athletic legs. He wears white socks, old boots on huge feet, a baseball cap, turned backwards. A backpack hangs off one arm. He drops it, stands the bike, removes his helmet, and then eases off with a kind of grace found only in hockey players and movie stuntmen. He revolves, and you see the shades over his eyes, the handsome face stubbled with five o'clock shadow, full lips that just beg to be kissed. He stretches and his T-shirt now rides up in the front, exposing a fur-ringed belly button and ripped midriff muscles. The meaty bulge in his shorts shifts hypnotically.

Your mouth transforms into desert. You forget to blink until your eyes start to burn. You've stopped breathing, too—that last sip of air boils in your lungs. Your heart revolts and you blink, swallow, breathe. In addition to these reawakened sensations, you realize that your cock is harder than you remember it getting in recent months. Or is that years? So hard, it aches. You reach down and squeeze hold of it. Unable to resist, you masturbate, using the copious precum leaking from its tip for lubrication.

The man—you peg him as being in his midtwenties—squats down to fish something out of his backpack: keys. You imagine what it must be like between those hairy knees and inner thighs; the smell of ripe balls, sweaty ass, musty dick...he must be gloriously hairy there, one would assume, given the state of the rest of his visible flesh. The stolen glimpse between his spread legs is all too fleeting; holstering his backpack, he marches up the stairs to the front door and out of sight behind the line of evergreens you put in fifteen or so years ago that smell like cat piss, junipers or yews, you don't remember which. He's gone from view, leaving you hard and gasping for breath, having the nearest thing to a religious experience you've ever known.

A god has just moved in next door.

The load you blast into a discarded sock verges on painful due to its intensity. It's been a while since you recycled your own junk, but this night you do, licking the pale, tasteless clots off the toes of the stale white cotton, pretending it's *his* batter. His, you know, would taste powerful, high-octane, musky. Alive.

Wonder of wonders, you worked up a sweat while beating your meat at the kitchen window. It's the heart of August, you work for that hardware giant, the one you and the guys at work jokingly call "Home Despot," and you can't remember the last time you got this thoroughly damp. A good case of the sweats usually comes about when the body attempts to flush something toxic out of its systems. You don't have a cold or fever, but there's an illness just as detrimental floating through your blood:

entropy. Soaked in perspiration, you take a shower, masturbate again and emerge feeling energized.

Too awake to sleep, you mosey back to the TV room at the back of your house. The television is still running, showing some cracked reality show, shit that will be forgotten by the masses the morning after its broadcast. In a world with such garbage passing for high culture, where everybody younger than you has a cell phone glued to his ear and most people don't know what planet they're on, is it any wonder you fell into this living coma?

You turn off the lamp and flip channels, finding a hospital drama from the early '80s you never watched then but for some reason do now. At least there's no hair pulling, ridiculous stunts, or panels of pissy judges and D-list celebrity hosts passing sentence on wannabe freaks.

So that's your new neighbor? The last tenants were an old couple, supremely quiet, who've since moved to Florida. There's a young, painfully handsome dude living there now. Rides a sport bike. Looks like he just flew down from Mount Olympus. You wonder if he has one of those trendy, low-hanging ball sac sort of names—Cody or Brody, Brendon or Brandon. They all sound like forbidden fruit. They all sound like poetry.

The night is late; it's already a few hours past your usual bedtime. A rare trip to your bedroom tonight seems your best bet. You kill the power on the TV; stand; pinch the tired corners of your eyes. But as you move through the dark toward the TV room's air conditioner and dial it down, you catch a ghostly shimmer of light in the top pane of glass, barely visible through the dense thatch of the sap pines behind both houses.

It's the light from the back bedroom next door. Your new neighbor's in there, perhaps stripping down for the night. Maybe having himself a little of that private pleasure you indulged in earlier. And it's a safe bet there aren't any curtains on those two windows just yet.

Ka-blam!

Lightning strikes again, jolting you back to the land of the living, and you remember what it was like to live, to lust, to risk everything for the reward of an unforgettable cheap thrill.

His name was Phillip McKinley. He was two years older than you and played on the high school baseball team. He once made you the brunt of an embarrassing public joke on the bus by offering you his slut of a girlfriend's lipstick. Made all the cool kids laugh, Phil did. Three years after you graduated, you would have thought you were his best pal, the way he waved to you whenever you drove past each other or met in the stores around town.

Thing was, you never really forgot what Phil did or forgave him for it. Then one rainy night, walking around the neighborhood feeling lost and horny, you happened to pass close to Dean Avenue, where Phil's family lived in an ugly split-level surrounded by towering spruce trees, and you decided to jerk it behind the safe cover of one of those giant evergreens. Remember your shock when, while basting your dick with spit, the fucker pulled up to the house in his secondhand sports car? Remember how life quickly spiraled out of control within the next few breathless minutes, minutes that felt more like hours in your paralysis, after a light snapped on in one of those downstairs rooms, Phil's bedroom, and you saw him strut into focus in all his macho-asshole glory, visible through the open Cape Cod curtains?

You snuck over, dick hard and flouncing with your steps, not thinking this was revenge, just hoping to see *something*. And did you ever! Phil, in his dirty bedroom, stripping out of his blue jeans and shit-kickers, down to a pair of checked boxers. Unaware there were eyes in the night tracking his moves, he peeled off his white crew socks, sniffed them. His boxers followed, baring an insanely hairy ass. Phil sniffed those, too. He turned on the tube and sprawled naked across the single bed. Reflected in the bureau mirror, you saw that he had turned the cable box to that old adult movie channel, hoping the signal would unscramble long enough for him to see something.

A former high school jock just starting to show the makings of a college beer gut, he was still magnificent to behold, with his long, furry legs and huge feet spread so close to the window-sill, you swore you could smell them; his handsome face and the mustache he no doubt imagined tickling a pussy or two with, his average-sized cock and above-average balls, hairy and apparently itchy, given the amount of tugging and scratching he showed them. Your dick, you saw with understandable pride, was bigger than Phil's. Big man on campus, your left nut! Skinny and hirsute, with a fireman's helmet already weepy with cloudy tears, it was a succulent mouthful, but no major league slugger.

What he did with it amazed you. How he slapped it back and forth, between his forefinger and thumb, a teasing action that eventually made Phil's balls pull up tightly around the root of his shaft and his head pop. You heard his grunts, but smartly contained your own. He sprayed his batter across his hairy chest and mopped it up with his shorts, farted, and passed out scratching his nuts in front of the tube. You blasted most of yours against the house's foundation. One shot, you noticed the next night, struck the window screen.

Oh, yes, you went back so many nights after that, watching Phil McKinley beat off while lurking in the darkness outside his bedroom window. Your inner voyeur, a sleeper agent until the night spent masturbating behind the spruce tree, had been acti-vated. Deactivating it would be a long time coming.

Staring across the backyard at your new neighbor's bedroom lights has brought that secret agent out of the past and into your present. A lusty smirk spreads across your lips. You lick them, taste something sweet. Your breaths are short and shallow, your bone steely and hot, and your sac feels like molten flesh, as though your nuts have liquefied. Thoughts of Phil McKinley fade—it's all about the new guy.

Your heart races, drumming in your ears. A new adventure. Fresh danger. You'd almost forgotten what it feels like to be this human.

Your backyard is accessible through the sliding glass door of the TV room, then it's down your deck to the grass and that line of hedges that stink of cat piss and end in dense sap pines. More pines and lots of scrub brush separate the rear of the property from the other houses one road over. It's very dark. Very private.

The house next door sits on a slope, the backyard overgrown from the house sitting vacant all these summer months. Flagstone patio leads to a screen door; bedroom windows, two of them. The air conditioner runs in one of those windows, masking the sough of your steps.

Wearing a shirt and loose-fitting shorts, no underwear to restrain your junk, and sneakers, you pad down your deck, your throat desiccated. Eyes wide and unblinking, you cross your yard, reach the trees, sneak through them. You're into the neighbor's yard before a mosquito buzzes your face. The body is older, but the cells don't really forget—you don't swat at it. Doing that will only attract its friends and potentially alert the handsome biker inside the house to your presence.

Cock aching, *dripping*, you approach the window. The overgrown grass tickles your bare ankles. Your new pal, that little bloodsucking bitch, sips at your neck, right near the hairline. You don't swat, you squash. You pull back damp fingers, which could be from blood or sweat. It's so damn hot out. The night smells like everything is cooking: primal, passionate, alive!

Closer, closer yet...

You've come to this house dozens of times, sometimes for barbeques, others to help out the former tenants who rented the place for almost a decade. Never did you think you'd be dropping in for this reason. You don't care. You're there.

At some point during the day, your new neighbor apparently moved in boxes and furniture. A dresser and bed—mattress and box spring, no headboard—fill the room. He's tossed a sheet over the bed, but it isn't tucked in. Creeping toward the window, you see his old motorcycle boots, sitting near the dresser. His white socks hang over their tops. At first, you're so consumed with thoughts of how magnificent they must smell that you don't see the other boots.

Boots: tall, polished jackboots, their shine eventually draws your focus. They rest beneath a two-dimensional effigy of a man, a dark and crisp man made of fabric with no head or limbs. It's a uniform. A policeman's uniform, dangling from a hanger. Your new neighbor, judging by his boots and colors, is a motorcycle cop.

A mix of fear and arousal flares through your blood at this realization.

You catch a shadow of movement from beyond the open bedroom door. The young god Phaeton strides in, dressed only in a bath towel cinched low around his waist. He's babbling into a cell phone. He scratches at his balls with his free hand. His hair is wet, and his naked chest glistens. Fresh from the shower, he is a vision almost too painful to behold with mortal eyes.

The buzz of another mosquito, or it could be the first, drones away. You whip out your cock, run your thumb over the head, swabbing juicy precum over the sensitive underside and pump, aware in a disconnected way that you're doing it the way you saw Phil McKinley bring himself pleasure, by spanking it up and down, back and forth.

He's got a million-dollar smile on his face that shows a length of perfect white teeth. That chest, with its T-pattern of dark fur, those legs, and his amazing feet, gigantic, with long toes, each capped by threads of shiny black hair…oh, how you long to lick each and every inch of his body!

The young police officer chuckles. Quite clearly over the roar of the air-conditioning unit that drips liquid as steadily as your cock, you hear him bellow, *"Dude!"*

Then he unhooks the towel, and it drops to his hairy ankles. Very little is clear after that, save for the image of the god's dick, a thick, flaccid tube of meat hanging out of a nest of dark curls over enormous, steam-loosened balls. He pulls on his cock, ogles his nuts. As you pump your tool outside, inside he jumps on the bed, still talking on his cell phone. The image of his soles nearly pushes you over the edge. He massages his balls. His cock unfurls out of its softness and swells. The fucking thing quickly grows past the eight-inch range, you swear. It would make you choke, but you'd gladly sputter all the way down to his bush.

The dude arches one leg. His balls spill down, cutting off your brief glimpse at his asshole. That wink of pink, however short, is enough for you to see his pucker is encircled by scruff. You love a hairy asshole, could eat one for hours and never grow tired.

He says good night to whoever's at the other end of the line, flips the phone shut and tosses it onto the empty side of the mattress. From there, the young god leans back, tossing one arm behind his head, half closes his eyes and starts masturbating.

The way he pumps his cock is pure poetry. The curl on his lips is more snarl than smile; part of you wishes you could invade his private thoughts as much as his private space to sample his jerk-off fantasies firsthand.

His balls pull up around his root. His toes curl. The head and top third of his shaft, gliding between his fingers, turn a fiery shade of crimson. He grunts a litany of expletives and, while you squirt your load into the weeds, he shoots four steady shots of whitewash over his hairy chest.

You've come three times tonight, which is three more than you planned to milk out of your balls. But you're not done yet. Back in your bedroom, gasping for breaths that refuse to come easily, you'll relive the last thing you saw before your new neighbor turned out the lights and caused you to flee: him, dragging his fingers through all that luscious chest hair and goo and then licking them clean.

You pass out, heart galloping, cock sore and itchy. Your mosquito bites leave you digging at your flesh. You just can't get that insanely powerful image of the motorcycle cop slurping on his own taste out of your head. Fucking hot. Fucking narcissist—a typical straight young stud so in love with himself, he eats his own spunk rather than allow it to go to waste.

The alarm sounds too early. You stagger sore and itchy into the bathroom to piss and brush your teeth, fighting the familiar paranoia gripping you for the first time in almost twenty years, since that last night outside Phil McKinley's house in the old neighborhood so far away from this one, where you've lived your safe and colorless existence.

You want to jerk off in the shower, but you don't. You towel dry, dress, drink your coffee, feel the weight of routine and boredom pressing down upon you. Last night's adventures are no longer real, but a dream. Someone else's dream, not yours. You have an hour before your shift begins. You always show up early. It's just another day, identical to so many others.

But then the doorbell rings.

Nobody ever visits you this early in the morning. Almost nobody ever visits, regardless what time of the day it is.

The vision that stands on the front stoop is impossibly bright, as if forged from morning sunlight, and also impossibly cruel in its beauty. The uniform badge pinned to the young deity's chest glows silver, not merely reflecting the light of the sun but seeming to harness it. This son of Apollo, God of War, and the nymph Clymene has been reborn and is in control of the elements.

"Hey, dude," he says in that jocular voice. *Dude.* You're one of his buddies now, even though you've only just met. His cocky smirk flashes that length of white teeth.

You open your mouth to respond, but the young man's perfect, dark brush cut, his crisp police uniform, those shiny boots, hold you transfixed. Suddenly, you're out of body, watching the exchange from an askew angle, drinking in this supernatural visitation the gods have blessed you with through your eyes as well as your soul.

"Sorry, didn't mean to spook you," the deity chuckles.

Thumb tucked into his gun belt, he offers the other hand to you; the same hand you watched him beat off with. The same set of fingers he used to scoop up his own batter for a nasty, salty late-night snack.

"I just moved in next door." He tips his chin, freshly shaved, toward the little ranch house beyond the stinking hedge. "I'm Steve Ranley."

He's not a Cody or a Brody, a Brendan or a Brandon, but his name still sounds like poetry.

The apparition version of you hovering in the doorway realizes you're staring and gives you a swift kick in the can. You tell him your name and extend your hand. You shake. The strength in the young policeman's hand verges on painful, though you couldn't love it more. In fact, you don't want to let go, afraid that when you do, you'll lick your palm and fingertips in front of him, even knowing he's since washed his hand, showered away all traces of DNA and musk. Somehow, you regain composure.

"The guy I rent from says you're a reliable dude, the guy in the neighborhood everybody counts on and trusts."

Guilt, sour and heavy, squirts through your bloodstream.

"Hey, if it's not any trouble, I have to get my ass in gear for my shift, but I got the cable dude coming sometime in the next three hours. I need someone to be there to let him in. Any chance you'll be home around eleven?"

"Yes," flies out of your mouth before you can censor it. "Sure, not a problem."

"Dude, you're a fuckin' lifesaver. If I don't get some tube, miss the baseball game again, I'm gonna go ape."

He claps your shoulder. Your flesh ignites, the zombified cells stimulated into feeling again.

"I left the back door unlocked, so if you could make sure it's shut up nice and tight after he's done…"

"You got it, Officer Ranley," you say.

Officer *Nice and Tight*—your eyes lock on his ass, which is magnificently firm, almost square around the edges in his uniform pants—revolves to face you.

"My friends call me Steve, dude."

"Steve," you sigh.

Glancing down, you see the expanding wet spot at the front of your blue jeans and worry that you might come at the open door, in clear view for the entire world to see. Luckily, you live on a dead-end road, two houses from a wall of tall pines, and the only witness beside the squirrels and birds has his back to you.

You step inside and close the door, unable to calm your galloping heart. The roar of the deity's crotch rocket launches a cannonade of thunderclaps through the hot morning air. Your inner critic absently wonders how long it will take the other neighbors to complain about the noise. The rest of you shivers at the powerful image of him, Phaeton atop his chariot, streaking past in a blaze of fiery light. So magnificent, so powerful and male, you don't realize you climax without so much as touching yourself, mistaking the icy-hot jolts through your body for hosannas in the highest, until you feel something hot and clotted running down your pant leg.

You call in sick. They give you attitude, which you find galling, considering your last sick day was almost two and a half years ago, a Christmas cold. You missed exactly one shift—you suffered through the next day on your feet, mostly without complaint. You're a good worker, always early, always willing to cover shifts when other drones fail the hive. *Fuck them,* you think. And then you repeat the sentiment out loud.

You strip out of your jeans, peel off your tighty-whities, stunned by the knowledge you've experienced your first nocturnal emission in three decades while awake. Granted, life for you has become one great big somnambulant episode, but it does feel like your body is coming to spring following winter; to life after a waking coma.

Steve. Stevie. Steven. Just saying his name's permutations, conjugations, *masturbations* puts a wide, dopey smile on your face. The world has again become a vivid, mysterious realm, a land of myths and legends, of gods and passions.

Dressed in new underwear and the same loose-fitting cotton shorts from last night's recce, you exit your house through the sliding glass door and tromp across the overgrown Elysian fields that separate your backyard from his, to await the cable guy.

In a daze, you enter the house. You've been here before plenty of times, know the lay of this land as clearly as your own home. The back door opens on a little mudroom; oblong second bedroom to your right, master bedroom to your left. Directly ahead is open space—living room, dining area, kitchen. The head is a few steps from the master, at the far left of the house. A simple 1960s ranch, identical to yours minus the upgrades you've made over the years.

Only it isn't the same house anymore. Sunlight streams through the curtainless windows in glittering columns. Boxes and bags and mismatched furniture—leftovers from childhood through early college frat house, with some curbside rescues thrown in—fill the place. This is the deity's lair now. A pizza box sits on the counter, along with a trio of empty fallen soldiers. The air conditioner is off, and the day's heat has started to bake the place. You smell a hint of beer from the drained longnecks, sweet and hypnotic. And something else, bitter around the edges: Foot odor. His.

Walking, your own feet never seeming once to touch the floor, you glide into the bedroom. His old motorcycle boots and the sweaty socks draped over both tongues are there, right where you saw them through the window glass. You lower. Withdraw them. Sniff the discolored cotton, right at the toes. That scent, along with ripe, sweaty balls, is a real man's smell. You find Officer Steve's dirty boxer-briefs in the bathroom, in a pile kicked into the corner, and take a deep whiff of those, too. Heavenly distraction!

You fall into the pull of powerful emotions—the strength in his handshake, the memory of him eating his own potent swimmers, the stink of his feet on those dirty socks—and lose track of time, of space. A paradox twists the two Universal Standards. Suddenly, you're inside his bedroom, sprawled across the bunched bedclothes, jerking on your dick while smelling the young god's dirty socks, but you're also outside, staring in. You're on both sides of the window.

Your eyelids fly open. Time and space untwist. It isn't some ghostly afterimage of you left over from the night imprinted on the day wandering around out there; it's the cable guy, looking for the junction.

The work order is for the big new flat screen in the living room and the older console unit in the bedroom. You leave a little love note to Officer Steve, editing out all the romance.

Cable all set.

You also, reluctantly, leave his socks.

It wasn't your intention to pass out on the sofa, watching a marathon of an old science fiction series on the tube. But you didn't sleep last night, and naps are sometimes a reality and a necessity of your age.

The doorbell rings.

Mouth stuck together with a foul taste, eyes almost plastered shut, you stagger out to answer the jarring gong. The odd angle of the light tells you it's late in the afternoon. You open the door and are again struck by how your visitor seems to control the sun, not the other way around. A fiery red aura encompasses Steve Ranley's muscular frame.

"Dude, thanks," he says in that jocular, buddy-buddy tone. "Couple zillion channels in high def, but as long as I have the one that airs tonight's baseball game, I'm happy."

"You're welcome," you manage to answer. "My pleasure to help out."

"You got anything going on? Wanna watch the game, share a couple of cold ones?"

Tiny, unseen explosions spark within you, a smaller version of the Big Bang that first gave life to the universe all those billions of years ago. You find your voice through the cacophony and a mouthful of invisible cotton and say, sure, you'd like that. What time? Long enough for him to get out of his uniform, grab a shower? Sure that works. You'll see him then.

It strikes you as he walks away that you're obsessed with the man, and this can only end one way: with you getting hurt. Possibly destroyed. It's happened before. But the knowledge does little to dampen your euphoria and so, for the next forty or so minutes, you pace the house, thinking only that the deity has smiled down upon you.

"Place is a mess, but you know that," he chuckles.

You manage some witty response about your house looking like a twister's gone through, even on the best of days, so not to worry. Of course, that's a lie. You keep things orderly, bordering on immaculate. It's part of the apathy you've fallen into. Order is safe. Pizza boxes on the counter and empty longnecks are a sign of chaos and the looming apocalypse.

He has showered but not shaved. Five o'clock scruff prickles across his chin, cheeks and neck. He's wearing an old T-shirt that bears the logo and the name of the same team you'll both root for following the first pitch. Luckily, you've masturbated to enough baseball games to know the intricacies of the team, the sport. You always liked baseball, but you sure bone the fuck up at the sight of the players.

Steve hands you a longneck. "You play?"

"Me, at my age? You kidding?" you chuckle.

"You're only what, early thirties?"

He says this with a look of seriousness on his handsome mug. You're in the very last of the years that can be classified as your early forties, and will soon have entered the middle time of your fourth decade's run. Living in a state of entropy has its advantages, apparently; all that formaldehyde in your blood has at least pickled you into appearing younger than you really are. You get a little chill, a nice stroke of the ego, from the compliment. The smile on your face is the first genuine one you've felt in...

"That's right," you lie. "Thirties."

He knocks back a sip and you try not to watch his throat, hairy with stubble, knot under the influence of a heavy swallow. You fail. The room takes a brief spin. "I'll play on the policeman's summer league next year. I'm sure there's pickup football in a month, probably hoops, too."

The shorts he wears, a pair of cargo pants with big pockets hacked off at the knees, showcase his incredible legs. He's wearing old sneakers, no socks, and you know for a fact how funky the insides must be with his natural, musty scent. The beer already makes you light-headed—when's the last time you ate anything? You're not much of a drinker to begin with. Not quite a lightweight, but close enough, and you worry you'll slip up again—toss wood, frottage yourself into a big old sloppy orgasm right in the middle of the second inning at the sight of his hairy calves, or if he continues to scratch absently at his nuts, or if he bends over and you catch the top of his underwear and perhaps a length of bare back when his shirt rides up.

Thing is, this former military guy who tells you he fought overseas seems genuinely nice. Phaeton might have been the son of a Greek god, but he was also part human. Though you lust for the deity you also like the dude.

"So, you married?"

The lightning bolt that cleaves you in half launches your consciousness out of your body, casts it to the ceiling, and leaves it clutching at the plaster while your corpse sits paralyzed. Forcing your lips to open takes a Herculean effort.

"Not yet. What about you?"

He shrugs, scowls, and the way his skin wrinkles around his eyes adds another layer of attraction to the whole. "Nothing serious, yet. Just moved here—give me a couple of days to notch the old bedpost, buddy."

Steve chuckles, smiles, but there's a hint of nervousness about his gestures.

"I'm sure it won't take you long," your body says, that idiot collection of lumped parts. Your soul, stuck on the ceiling, pleads for you to stop, to cease and desist from going further. "Stud like you, you'll be fighting them off with your police baton."

You chuckle, too, and your consciousness hates the sound of it.

Steve shoots you a look.

"No doubt," he says. But you can see it in his gaze, that spark of *Eureka!* that wasn't there before. The light has dawned on Marblehead. He's invited a cocksucker into his house. A genuine, boner-fide, ball-licking, spunk-slurping homosexual. "Thanks, man," he says, finishing his beer.

His eyes drill into yours, so blue they appear to glow with a preternatural glint. Your soul tumbles off the ceiling, plummets awkwardly back into your body, which feels all bumps and gristle.

"Until that pussy parade begins," he says, "it's nice to have made a friend in the neighborhood."

He raises his empty. Your paralysis breaks. You chime bottles together, not sure what to think or believe, only that life has become supremely interesting—and terrifying—in the past handful of hours.

The hometown team loses the game, and every one of Steve's bellowed swears when a player strikes out or a well-hit ball doesn't go the distance, dying in the humid air and falling into an opposing player's glove, threatens to either stop your heart or stiffen your dick. Most of you can't wait to get out of there, while the rest never wants to leave.

"Fuckin' bullshit," he grumbles, putting that final stamp on the evening.

You agree. "At least it's only one of a hundred and sixty-two games."

"Still," he sighs. "Thanks for coming over and hanging out, dude."

"Pleasure was mine." You shake hands, worried some of your bones are going to snap. "We should do it again."

"Yeah, dude, for sure."

"I have a mean grill on my deck. Maybe get some steak action going—if you have the time."

"Time?"

"You know, once that whole pussy parade starts."

"Oh, that. I'll let you know."

He says *Later,* and you head out his front door, into the blast furnace. The outside light feels like a spotlight, marking your walk of shame back to the house. As you cross the lawn, aware of the hollow, sinister sound of the sunburned grass beneath your sneakers, your heart begins to hammer in your chest. You enter through the front door but don't turn on any lights. The bright beacon next door snaps off.

Struggling to breathe, you cross through the house on memory, make it to the sliding glass door, your flesh on fire, your blood rabid with raw, sexual excitement. Out the sliding door, onto the deck, you arrive in time to see the back bedroom's light snap on over at Steve's house. The humid, milky sky and the wall of the surrounding trees mask your presence; the roar of the AC window unit, your steps. You cover the distance doing a dogtrot, light-headed. It could be the beer or your blood pressure, rising in anticipation of what you hope you'll see. You move through the trees, over the weeds, to the window.

You reach your destination right as Steve drops trou, baring that incredible ass that eluded you previously. He squats down, pushing shorts and boxer-briefs to his ankles. Bloated balls dangle beneath a fur-ringed bullet hole, and you gasp at the unholy lust that possesses you. You would eat his hairy pucker deeper than any asshole in the history of all assholes. So deep, you shudder in spite of the heat.

Steve straightens, revolves. His cock juts out ahead of him, not entirely hard but only a few firm strokes shy. He scratches his balls, tugs on his tube. Yawns. Even the lush, dark nests of fur under his pits are the stuff wet dreams are made of.

There's a beer bottle in the room, identical to the two you drank, the three he knocked back. Perhaps it's the last of a six-pack. Naked, with his cock flouncing, Steve carries it over to the bed, two long fingers wrapped around its neck in that classic he-man stance. He takes a swig from the bottle, sets it beside the bed, hops onto the mattress, turns on the bedroom TV.

You fumble out your dick, conjure spit from the desert that your mouth has degenerated into and lube your erection. You start to jerk off. In the room, so does the deity, the dude. There's so much to watch that your eyes don't know where to focus, so they dart over his big, naked feet and those sweaty toes you ache to suckle, his legs, his balls, his cock. Your mouth waters at the notion of gently nipping the dime-sized hard points of his nipples. You'd give anything to shove your nose into his armpits and take a deep, moist whiff. The thought of actually kissing Steve Ranley's lips carries unexpected consequences, sending you over the edge, making you piss your wad all over the weeds. Biting back the howls, the excitement crashes over you, leaves your legs weak. Sweat cascades out of your hair and into your eyes.

You shake out your cock, tuck it away, zip up. You've had more than enough fun for one night both inside the house with Steve and outside, watching him beat off. *Quick—go home!* The voice in your thoughts tells you to run. But Steve is still jacking on his dick, and you can't look away, not yet. What if he does that little recycling trick again? Can't miss that. Tired as you are, your knees threatening to buckle, you keep watching. And watching.

He rewards you with yet another surprise, this fine young man who has taken a vow to uphold the law you're presently breaking. He reaches for the beer bottle, downs a hearty gulp of suds, then places the sweating longneck on his crotch, lining it up beside his shaft. Smiling proudly to himself, the young god revels at how his dick and the beer bottle match in height and almost width at the thickest point of the glass. Using both hands, he pumps them together, up and down, masturbating his cock against the cold, wet bottle. This image drives your dick back to the consistency of stone. Hauling it out, you see stars. The stars burn down to little black dots before your eyes. You rapidly blink them away, not wanting to miss a moment of what's to come.

Up and down, the action jiggles the bottle. A head of foam

oozes up and out of the spout, congealing between Steve's fingers. He uses it for lube—beer suds and precum. Your mouth waters for a taste. The motion hypnotizes you.

He squirts a jet of ball-juice up and over the beer bottle, striking his chin. His tongue darts out and catches some of it. Another salvo rips across his chest. The rest sprays the beer bottle's exterior. Sweat pours down the policeman's face, now stained a deep shade of crimson along with his neck and the top of his chest.

Do it, you silently urge. *Fuckin' do it, dude!*

And, as if hearing your plea, he lifts the beer bottle to his lips, chugs down the suds, and then he licks the goo dripping down the sweating bottle and sucks the cocktail of cum and suds off his fingers.

You lose it, busting your second nut of this strange and wonderful night against the side of his house.

In the darkness, you toss and turn, feeling dirty, processing all that you've learned: Steven Ranley is a rookie police officer, rides a chopper, is former Army, loves baseball, beer and the taste of his own spunk. Steven Ranley is insanely handsome, and you're obsessed with him. There, it's all out in the open. Or as open as the dark confines of your bedroom allow.

You lie in a fetal curl with a smile on your face, giddy that he has snuck into your little sheltered life here on a dead-end street, because it doesn't feel so dead with him around. Granted, you've now spent the past two nights peeking through his bedroom window, watching him do that thing men do best, but there's a level of intimacy in the action. It's yours and his and no one else's.

Your inner critic taunts you with thoughts of that whole "old cat/new kitten" analogy, about a young pet bringing out the last gasp of youth from an elderly one. But you shut its yap with a warning. You're not old, not elderly. And you don't know exactly what these feelings are, good or bad, only that you're happy to feel something, anything.

You haven't been intimate with another guy for a while. The last one was a come-and-go married dude from one town over you met online, with a great average-sized cock that refused to ejaculate, even though you did your best to make it spray. After a few hours of licking his balls and asshole and bringing yourself to climax, he confessed his high blood pressure meds often led to this result at home with the wife, ergo his curiosity to try something different to get off, like receiving a blow job from another man. You both lost interest after that and gave up, and though you never voiced it outright, you thought it: this was the end of the line for you regarding sex. The dead end. Or so you thought.

Throughout the night, you wake to sounds like the roar of his sport bike, that hot crotch rocket fuck-machine, and from dreams that you're on the seat with him, Phaeton, son of Apollo, your arms wrapped around his waist, one hand on his stomach, the other cupping his balls. Then you catch a flash of lightning across the bedroom wall and realize the summer has turned violent.

Awake now, you remember what happened that night outside Phil McKinley's house when you got caught, why you moved so far away from the old neighborhood, and why you might yet be forced to move from this one if you stay on this present path.

Morning: You go through the motions. Take your shower. Dress. You grab your bottle of soda, your apron and name tag and head out the door, locking it behind you. The previous night's rain hasn't cooled the day, just stirred up the scent of summer. Mowed grass, the last crop of summer blueberries ripe on their bushes, pine trees, and tea roses, all cooking together, the fragrance seasoned by the humidity. It's seductive and sensual; you ignore it and head to your car, hoping you'll get there and be gone before—

The clarion sounds, as Phaeton kicks the chariot's heart into gear. The blast of his motorcycle coming alive echoes over the neighborhood. You hop behind the wheel of your sport utility vehicle, hoping you haven't been seen. Dear god, not again. You can't take the passion, the danger, the happiness or the hurt.

The young policeman glides into your driveway, parks the bike directly behind you, cutting off your escape. It's too late. You're trapped. You glance into the rearview and can't believe the image that greets your eyes: Steve Ranley, jumping off his motorcycle, big jackbooted feet marching over to the driver's-side door. He raps his gloved knuckles on the window glass the same way he would with speeders and other lawbreakers. Your heart jumps. Criminal, you've been found out, unmasked.

You lower the window. The face that greets you is too handsome for mortals to behold directly. He's worse than a Gorgon or Medusa—you won't turn into stone by facing Phaeton directly, you'll burst into flames.

"Dude," he says. "How about we enjoy those steaks tonight?"

It isn't Steve Ranley there for an instant, but Phil McKinley. Your jaw erupts with the memory of exquisite agony. The flesh never really forgets, does it?

"Can't," you say. "Gotta work late. Sorry."

"That sucks. How about we hang later, then?"

Lying only digs your grave deeper. "Inventory tonight, dude."

"Well, maybe tomorrow."

"Yeah, maybe."

He drives off and you curse yourself in silence, hearing the drone of the motorcycle as it fades into the distance down your pleasant, boring road where nothing much used to happen. The rabid creature infecting your blood begs you to go after him; when you don't, it attempts to hold on to the echo of gears, torque, testosterone, as if that noise had a physical body. Then the echo is gone completely, and you know the angry presence inside you is going to make you suffer for denying it that which it craves most.

Him.

Throughout the course of a long gray day, you smile on the outside and your soul dies a little more with each passing hour. You help customers and coworkers, some of them so bitchy and repellent that you can feel the life force draining from you, sucked out of your pores and absorbed by their miserable hides.

You take your lunch in the break room and, for the very first time, realize how bland the human landscape is. You're not friends with any of your coworkers, not in the way knowing Steve seems to be redefining the word's meaning. None of these people ever invite you over for beer and baseball games or ask to share steak dinners with you. You've known the deity next door for only a pair of days and nights, and yet he already feels more substantive to your world than these living ghosts.

You pick up an additional ninety minutes of OT, until the night supervisor literally boots you out of the store. You sit in your SUV, fogging up the windows, listening to the driving rain pelt the roof and windshield. It was raining that night, too. The night Phil McKinley caught you outside his bedroom window. Rarely do you ever revisit that memory—it occupies a singularly terrible and foggy place in your past that came with far-reaching consequences. You clamp down on the thoughts before too many of them come tumbling through the closet door inching open in your mind's eye.

You head to the local big chain bookstore, sip a cold coffee drink that'll leave you wired for the rest of the night, for sure. Flip through a modern volume of Ancient Greek mythology. Relive the stories of Orpheus and Eurydice, Tantalus and cursed Phaeton. You wonder if the game got rained out and, if so, what the lonely young god is up to. And if he isn't with you, who is he doing things with?

A whole new layer of worry gets heaped onto the shit storm torturing you in silence. Maybe Steve is making new friends. Or friends who fuck. Half of you panics that he'll move on, because you were such a cold fish this morning in the driveway. You genuinely enjoyed hanging out with him...so what if all you ever end up being is buddies, dudes? Isn't that enough?

The other half, the dark side, says no in an emphatic tone. You've watched the rookie policeman masturbate. You know some of his secrets—such gloriously filthy, wonderful secrets; ones that will fuel your own fantasies for the remainder of your life. You've spied on him during his most private and sacred moments. There's danger in that kind of knowledge, and though you suffered for similar trespasses a very long time ago and were able to get away mostly intact, this time the risk could cost you more than a bashed-in cheek and a ton of humiliation.

You gaze at the clock. Christ, it's after nine and you feel like you've been away from home for an eternity. You drive the distance through the lashing rain. The rain's the real culprit here. You were mostly okay until the heavens opened up, killing the illusion that you were coming back to life, that you and Steve Ranley could have *something* together, by conjuring memories of Phil McKinley and a night that should have remained buried in history.

Another specter rises up to haunt you on the drive home, a voyage that seems to take far longer than it should: will there be another car parked in Steve's driveway? Another motorcycle? Another dude?

Heart in your throat, you drive, barely able to see the pavement in the rain. The mist that swirls among the darkened pines at the dead end of your road obscures almost everything. Steve's driveway, however, sits empty. You race into the house, getting soaked to the skin. Turning on only the kitchen light, you plod into the TV room and glance out the window that faces toward Steve's house. The ghostly electric glare of the TV is barely visible through the trees and the downpour. Rainy nights, they were the best ones to catch your horny neighbor-dude beating off, the one who humiliated you with his girlfriend's lipstick, your dark side thinks. Well, most nights, anyway.

The temptation to go out there, perhaps catch Steve stroking his dick to a dirty movie or playing with his balls or picking his sweaty toes or just sleeping with an angelic corona of television light around his magnificent face tempts you. But you stop yourself before reaching the sliding glass door.

Calmly, quietly, you strip out of your wet clothes and crawl into bed, not bothering to turn on the air conditioner, not caring that the air in the room is hot and stale, or the sheets need changing, or that each *plink* of a raindrop against the windowpane threatens to take you back to that long-ago night. Your mind drifts, and you wonder about Steve. How is he? Is he lonely? Who is he thinking about on this melancholy night?

Back to entropy.

You avoid Steve, rearranging your schedule.

Leave earlier in the morning than he does.

Get home later at night.

Don't masturbate, climb walls.

Obsess about all that you know:

Rookie cop. Ex-Army. Two tours in Afghanistan.

Police academy after service.

Single.

Eats own sperm.

Beautiful.

For days, every time you hear the roar of the chopper, one part of you comes alive, while another retreats from living.

Fucking life.

One day, no different than the next.

August ends.

September begins.

And then, one night, as you drive down the road...

Two cars in the driveway next door greet your eyes. It's an early September evening, still warm, but you know it is the end of summer. There's a hint of change in the air, a scent of autumn around the edges. You park your car, carry takeout into the house, expect you'll fall asleep in front of the TV, as you have so often lately. And you'll no doubt dream about riding with Steve on the back of his chariot, a recurring theme these many weeks.

Only now, you might not sleep. Not at all. Looks like the Greek god has brought down a few friends from Olympus. You hear a sharp titter of what sounds like drunken laughter through the TV room window, a woman's voice. The pussy patrol has arrived, it would appear. Steve's gonna fuck long and hard tonight.

Sweaty, steadily driven mad by the knowledge that a hot man and his hot lay are fucking like primitive savages next door, your eyes tick. You don't eat; you push your food around in the carton with a fork. You don't watch TV, just flip channels, supremely distracted. You gaze out the windows to see the light on in Steve's bedroom. You pace, masturbate for the first time in a week, and what comes out of you almost hurts when it's released. Your balls melt. Your aching cock refuses to go soft or be satisfied with simple fantasy—it craves visual stimuli.

Left with no clear option, you turn off the lights, drawn moth-like to the glow from next door. Heart racing, you're subservient to your lust once more. Your flesh tingles—you've become one massive, pulsating cock from head to toe.

Another girlish giggle sounds through the open window. Steve's taken out the AC unit and put up curtains since the last time, you discover. But the curtains sway in the gentle breeze, offering a mostly unobstructed view of the inside.

Steve lies sprawled across the bed with not one but *two* women. He's on the far left of the mattress, with a blonde sand-wiched between him and the bottle-redhead on the right. Red's got long curly hair and is fondling the blonde's shaved pussy. Steve's feeling up the blonde's tits. They all kiss in the middle.

You are shocked yet excited by what you see. Two women—it's every straight man's dream. Over the years, while surrounded by drywall and lumber, some of the tools at work, the knuckle-draggers you secretly fantasize about having forgettable one-night stands with, bragged about bagging two chicks at the same time.

Only this doesn't seem to be Steve's ultimate dream. His eyes are closed while he kisses, and there's another element, subtle yet glaring. Steve is down to his boxer-briefs. Gray ones. Both of his nuts hang full and swollen out one leg—freed, obviously, in the wild mutual pawing. But his cock hangs half-limp, concealed by cotton. You've seen this guy toss serious wood that's hard enough to bang nails into walls with over the prospect of simple masturbation. Here he is, with actual human women, *two of them*, and his dick's snoozing.

"What the fuck," you gasp, your voice softer than a whisper, almost nonexistent.

Steve's hand reaches toward the shaved pink opening already filled with fingers. You catch a look on his face, not quite a smile. His leg stretches out, rubs against the blonde's.

"Ouch, that stings! Your legs are so hairy," she gripes.

Steve withdraws his touch, as though his fingers have been singed. "Sorry," he says. Gives his balls a shake. Covers them up. His cock looks even limper. He slides off the bed.

"Where you going?" the redhead asks.

"You two keep at it. Me and my hairy legs need some air."

Panic infuses your blood, paralyzing you to the spot when what you need to do is run, dammit, *run!* Get the hell out of there. He hauls on his military cutoffs and is stuffing his big bare feet into his sneakers before you ever turn around and take that first all-important step toward home.

The back door squeaks open, bangs into place. Your entire body prickles, infected by terror, panic. Somehow, you make it to the line of pine trees, awkwardly hide behind a trunk, impaling yourself on the leftover point of a dead branch. It jabs you in the side, hard enough, you're sure, to draw blood. Sweat pours down your face, clings thickly to your underarms, your lower back. The low sough of the September breeze barely cools your skin. It can't disguise his exasperated sigh. You hear the shuffle of his sneakers, then furtive footsteps across the backyard's sod. Dear God, he's coming toward you!

Oh fuck-fuck-fuck!

Steve's big feet, normally so sexy to you, unleash terror through your blood; an icy shiver tumbles down your spine. Closer, closer yet...sure you're about to collapse and die at any second, you see him appear at the tree line, three pines down. There he stands, tragic son of the gods, cast out of Olympus to live among the human race. Heaven help you.

He marches across your back lawn and exhales again, an

exasperated sound; shuffles forward, closer toward the deck.
Life then takes a hell of an ironic turn, twisting into a theater of
the insane. He drags himself up one step, then another, makes
it to the door and glances into your TV room. He's a shadow
in the darkness, yet clear enough for you to see him tugging at
his crotch, pulling on his meat. He whips out his cock. It's hard
now. You watch in a daze as he strokes his erection. Strokes
it outside your door, peeking in. He grunts; untimed moments
later, he busts his load all over the glass.

Steve Ranley has just forsaken two horny babes with bisexual
tendencies to squirt his seed across your domain, as if marking
his territory. He shakes out his hose, tucks it back in. Tenta-
tively, he slinks down the deck, starts back in the direction of his
house, where the ladies still wait.

"Fuck, fuck, fuck," he grumbles, almost at the tree line,
now.

Boldly, you extricate yourself from the shadows, the impale-
ment. Step into view.

"Steve?"

Steve jumps in place.

"What the fuck?"

You dare not believe what you've seen, that this fine young
man, this god among humans, would want *you* so passionately;
that he would stare in at *you,* unable to curb his desire for *you.*
Impossible. Maybe you only hallucinated what you think you
saw.

"Hey," you say. Arms akimbo, your dick so hard, so big in
your pants, it feels like a fifth limb.

Steve gazes at you, his eyes wild and unblinking.

"What—?" he huffs. "What are you doing, dude? Watching
me, huh?"

And then a wild animal is upon you, knocking you to the

ground. The musky stink of its body fills your next shallow breath. The animal climbs on top of you, too powerful to fight off.

"Huh, man?" it bellows, its voice carrying across the neighborhood, rising loudly for all to hear.

Your heart readies to explode. It isn't an enraged Steve Ranley on top of you anymore, in the here and now—it's Phil McKinley. Barefoot, dressed in the shorts he wears while beating his meat that fateful rainy night. He happens to glance up, right at the precise moment the lightning flashes, and he sees you standing outside his bedroom window with your johnson in your hand. You turn to run, praying to whatever deity will listen to have mercy upon you. But a fleet-footed former jock tears out of his house, his cock hard, his macho anger fueled into the danger zone.

You race toward the street corner, hoping the tall spruces will mask your escape. Only there is no getting away. A powerful force tackles you to the ground. You land hard enough to see stars, blue stars, shaped like flames. Those little flickers of natural gas that used to ignite before your eyes when, as a young boy, you got a cold and coughed yourself miserable throughout the darkness of the night.

"What the fuck—?" Phil bellows into your face. He rolls you over and recognition dawns on his face, visible in the next flash of lightning. "*You?* What the fuck are you doing, trying to rob my house? You fuckin' lowlife fuck!"

"No," you gasp. The raw male stink of his flesh, his sweaty balls and musty armpits, overwhelms your better judgment. "It ain't like that, I swear!"

And then you reach up, ogle the hot, meaty fullness of his crotch, your fingers finding their way into his shorts, around his loose, sweating nuts, his spit-slick cock. You feel Phil tense on top of you, too stunned to react.

"It's *you* I want," you babble.

Hearing your voice breaks his paralysis. Often since, you've wondered that if you'd just kept silent, would he have let you jerk him off, suck his dick, drink the load that he probably never got to blast? Right before he clocks you, you hear him growling, possibly because he loves the way you tickle his hairy sac and pump his erection.

The rest passes in a savage blur: A punch to the jaw. A bitter, metallic taste on your tongue, as though you've just sucked on a mouthful of pocket change. His voice, a roar, calling you a fuckin' cocksucker, louder than a chopper's roar.

Phillip McKinley has returned. He's on top of you here, now, in your present. Angel of death. This time, there's no telling what his wrath might inflict upon you. It is now the end of your days.

The angel leans over you, only he's no angel, but a tragic Greek deity. Phaeton. Steve Ranley. Phil McKinley is long gone, has been for decades.

"Why, dude?" Steve asks, his voice softening with pain.

"Because...I think..." you stammer.

You reach up, touch Steve's hairy inner thigh, grope his meaty balls, tickle them.

"Yes?" he grunts, out of breath.

Your hand travels higher, into the swampy wetness surrounding his cock. You grip his thickness and squeeze.

"Because I love you, Steve," you say.

"Oh, fuck, dude," he sighs.

A wide, beautiful smile spreads across his stubbled lips. His breath, minty and warm, gusts down, over your face. You inhale his scent, revel in the sensation of touching his cock, freed from so many invisible chains, alive and absolved.

"Me, too," he whispers.

And then, wonder of wonders, he crushes his mouth over yours.

It starts right there on the ground, with a kiss. Perhaps the most spectacular kiss in the history of the world. His lips caress yours. His tongue tests your boundaries; you open, and he charges into your mouth. Steve takes gentle nips at your face around deep, hungry kisses.

You help him out of his shorts, lick his balls, suck each gently into your mouth, one at a time. When he urges you to keep going, you suckle harder, pumping on his cock the entire time. You lap at the smelly patch of skin behind his nuts before shoving your tongue up his asshole, swirling it around. He orders you to service his bone. You do.

And you kiss.

Kissing, bodies pressed together, he backs you up the stairs and into your house. In the darkness, you navigate the way to your bedroom. He tosses you onto the bed, falls beside you. Those feet—you beg him to let you savor them.

"My feet, dude?" he chuckles, obviously unaware of the vast sexual potential to be had in that part of a man's body.

But before this night is over, he will.

You worship his body. He samples yours, lets slip between his first orgasm and the third that when you opened your door that sunny August morning, you were the most attractive human being he'd ever seen, male or female. That *you* are what he fought for overseas, what he risks his life for every single day he puts on the uniform.

You make love for hours, fall asleep together spooning. When the alarm jolts you awake in the muddy early morning hours, the room smells of sweat, of sex between two men, of life.

Steve dresses and heads home. The driveway sits empty—both of his conquests have fled. It's only you and him now.

"How about those steaks tonight?" you ask.

"I'll be here, right after my shift. Look forward to it, babe."
He winks, snarls.

Babe. Hearing him say this makes it all so real. You're young
again. You've been reborn.

It's a beautiful sunny September morning. The game will be on
in a few hours. You've spent the early part of the day, among
other things, getting to know each other. One of the subjects
that has cropped up has been Steve moving out of the rental and
into your house. Another is motorcycles.

"Ever been on a bike before?" Steve asks.

"Never," you say.

He flashes you that cocky look you love so much. "Come
on."

Reluctantly, you mount the sport bike behind him, wrapping
your arms around his waist. The muscles of his back and his
spine rub your front. Sound explodes. Air rushes around you.
Your grip on him tightens. The fingers of one hand slink lower,
cupping his balls.

The sport bike tears down the road, though there's no way
it can stay on the upright and steady, you think. But suddenly,
you're flying. Flying with Phaeton, fondling his nuts, high on
his scent. You could still crash and burn together, die in a ball
of fire; only this time, the gods smile down upon you and the
sun embraces you both. Light engulfs your body and on you fly,
holding on to him, happier and more in love, more alive, than
you ever dreamed possible.

AND THEN, I HELD HIM TIGHT…

Mark James

S oon, when Sabrael gave us the light of a new day, I would
know a pleasure I had ached for, longed for, since my first
night in Romejin's furs.

My Master had taught me many ways to seduce and please a
man. But I was a virgin. "Master, why must this be my last time
in your furs?"

He pulled me close. "Tomorrow, before the Patrons, I will
open you, and then—"

His words broke off. I twisted in his arms, pressed my naked
body close, looked up at him. "Then what, Master?"

Romejin was silent for so long, I thought I had displeased
him, and I would be sent for his Training Whip. "Then things
will be as they should be," he said.

"But after the Opening Rites, I'll never feel your touch again.
Why does Sabrael forbid us to be together?"

He sprang up, paced the small chamber. "We live unnatural
lives, trapped inside the metal skin of a beast." He whirled to his

Training Whip hanging over his furs, ripped it down and flung it into a corner. "We are forced to obey a machine, a monster who knows nothing of love."

In three turns of Sabrael's Great Wheel, never had I seen my Master so angry. I slipped from his furs, knelt at his feet. "You speak dangerous words, Master." My voice was little more than a whisper. "Sabrael is all seeing, all hearing. He cares for us, protects us." I raised my eyes to him. "He punishes those who disrespect His name."

Romejin seemed to pull himself in, as though he'd been sprinting at top speed and now forced himself to a slow walk. He breathed deeply.

"No Serving Slave has ever stayed with his Trainer," I said. "It's Sabrael's way. I wanted only to know why."

He brushed my light yellow hair back from my eyes.

"There is another way, boy."

"How?" I kissed between his legs, pressed my face close. "How can there be anything else?"

Romejin swept me up into his arms, laid me on his furs, kissed my throat.

"Do you trust me, Nitesh?"

"With my life, Master."

"Then rest. And when the Rites are over, after I have opened you, hold me tight."

He laid my head on his shoulder, brushed his fingers up and down my back. His last words chased me across the borders of sleep. *If I could*, I thought, *I would hold you forever.*

When I woke, he was gone. I thought of going after him, but I saw his Training Whip coiled in the furs beside me. From my earliest times with him, he had taught me the lesson of that warning. If I crossed the whip, he would cross my back with lashes.

I lay thinking of Romejin's anger. I didn't understand it. Things were as they had always been. Long ago, Sabrael's teachings tell us, we came from a world called Earth. A disease spread there, a pandemic. Millions died.

Sabrael waited in space, built to explore. But in the Time of Desperation, our forefathers remade Him. Before they launched Him into deep space, they boarded with many more eggs than they would need to seed galaxies of worlds.

The eggs waited even now, for Sabrael to find our first home.

But Seekers whispered Forbidden Tales.

That Sabrael had gone mad; that He was determined to hurtle through space forever, growing men and slave boys in Birth Chambers, keeping us within His walls, immune to disease, forever safe. It was said that Seekers lived in the dark, that they gathered Believers, and one day they would fly through space in Sabrael's children, Life Boats to a new world. But living inside Sabrael, who knew even our most secret thoughts, seeking and believing were forbidden, dangerous dreams.

Sabrael had chosen the Endless Sea for the Opening Rites. We were on the dark wooden deck of a sailing ship so big, we were an island in the sea. Tall white sails billowed above us. Blue waves hit both sides in an easy rhythm, as though the ship had a slow heartbeat.

Patrons, Men of the High Castes—Ship Overseers, Law Keepers, Star Seers—lay on couches shaped like small ships. They were dressed in silks of gold, deep green, scarlet red, rich blue to match the sea. When the Rite was over, these men would be the first to use my newly opened body for their pleasure.

In the middle of the deck, a stage rose, covered in white furs. In the center of the furs lay my Master's Training Whip. I knelt naked at Romejin's feet. He towered over me, wearing only black silk trousers. He stood with his legs spread, hands behind him, his head inclined to the Patrons.

Twelve holograms of boys with their Masters ringed the deck, seeming to float on the calm seas. My Master's and my hologram hung just over our heads. I knew that throughout the thirteen Spokes of the ship, men gathered around life-sized holograms, watching the Opening Rite of the Serving Slave who would join their Pleasure Chambers.

Behind me, Romejin lowered himself to the furs. I yearned for the shelter of his shadow over my naked body. His words echoed through my mind. *When you are afraid, use your body to distract.* I spread my legs wider, arched my back, and knew eyes would be drawn away from the fear on my face.

Romejin trailed his fingers down my trembling body.

I tilted my head back, offered my lips to him.

He kissed me, slid a finger between the cheeks of my ass, teased my virgin hole.

Knowing all the men watching would hear every sound I made, see even my smallest movement, I moaned softly.

Romejin bent lower, slid his finger deeper into me.

I pushed back, writhed, showed the watching Patrons my aching need.

He ran his other hand down my body, lifted my balls, showed the precum seeping from my hard cock.

The Patrons made a low greedy sound. I knew at least one of them had to be thinking of how I would look, lying on my belly, squirming, grabbing the furs, while he plowed into my freshly opened ass. Romejin must have sensed my wandering thoughts. He sat back, spread his legs, rubbed his hand over the bulge straining against his trousers. "Tell us what you want, boy."

I licked my lips; left them moist, inviting, as he had taught me. "To feel you inside me, Master."

A ripple of surprise swept through the Patrons.

Too late I realized I'd spoken from my heart, not from my Master's feet, as the Serving Slave he'd trained me to be. He'd told me countless times, *a slave always waits, never directs a man to serve his needs.*

Romejin coiled the Training Whip around his big fist until only a length as long as my arm hung free. "No."

My heart thudded. It was hard to force my eyes away from his whip, to force myself to relax. If I tensed for the sting of the whip, ruined the pleasing lines of my body, I would get more than one lash; perhaps more than two. I fell back on his lessons, crawled as close as I dared, kissed his feet.

He twisted his thick fingers into my hair, pulled me up, forced my head back. "What is it you need, Nitesh?"

Desperate to avoid the sting of a lash here, under the hungry eyes of the Patrons, I struggled to be calm.

He ran a finger over my bottom lip. "Show us, boy."

All that he'd taught me about seducing a man flooded back. I kissed the fingers of his fist that held the whip, caressed his balls through his trousers.

Feeling the eyes of the Patrons on me, I kissed Romejin's hard belly, trailed my soft lips over ridges of muscle. I went lower, pulling his trousers down as I went.

He ran his whip down my back, let the soft leather trail over my bare skin.

I knew that if I displeased him again, I would have no warning before a caress from his whip turned into a lash that would bring me to tears.

Romejin shuddered, pressed my head down.

For a moment, I forgot the Patrons. I buried my face between his legs, sucked his heavy balls into my mouth and slid my tongue over them, under them, around them.

A hard press of his fist against my back, a reminder of the whip he held, a reminder of where we were, brought me back to the heartless reality; I had shared his furs for the last time. I knelt back, slid the tip of my tongue along the underside of his cock. Low murmurs ran through the Patrons. The boat rocked, as though we'd gone over a thousand tiny waves. Taking his slick balls in my hands, I ran my thumbs over their velvet softness. Romejin spread his legs wider, lifted his hips. I licked his swollen cockhead, closed my lips over his pisshole. He lifted my chin and tilted my head back, so he could take my mouth in one deep stroke.

Knowing that this time my reward would be what I'd begged for on so many nights, knowing I'd be his after waiting so long, aching to feel Romejin's hardness fill my virgin ass, I took him deeper in my throat than I ever had.

The cries of slave boys echoed across the water, as their Masters opened them with hard cocks deep in their virgin holes. The Patrons applauded softly at the cry of each boy.

I felt him in my mouth, hard and throbbing. What was he waiting for? Why didn't he open me? He thrust into me, pulled back, did it again and again. "Your turn is coming, boy," Romejin whispered.

It couldn't come soon enough. I didn't want to need him inside me so badly, but I did. The fear of being ripped from his side was all but drowned in my need to feel him sliding into me, opening my virgin tightness.

Another boy cried out. The Patrons applauded.

And then I understood. Romejin was waiting for me to be the last virgin. When he took me for the first time, when I felt his caresses for the last time, every eye in every chamber on the ship would be trained on us.

He dropped the whip, pulled me up onto his lap until I straddled him, his eyes locked on mine. He reached for the oil beside us, pressed two slick fingers into me.

I moaned, held on to his shoulders.

He slid his fingers in and out, waiting, making the Patrons wait for my cries. When I thought I could stand it no longer, he slid his fingers all the way out of me. In training, he had always stopped there, always come in my mouth, never held my hips as he did now, never guided me until his thick cock was pressed up against my virgin ass.

I bit my lips, felt the pain of him spreading me, opening me before my entire world. He leaned close, kissed me, slid his tongue over mine. Then he thrust up.

Pain seared deeper into me. I panicked, tried to pull back, but his iron grip held me. Then I felt something I'd never felt in any training—him, deep inside me, filling me. The pain dwindled until it was a dim red glow inside the pleasure of being taken by my Master. He felt me give in to him and relaxed his hold on me.

I wanted to beg him not to ever let go, to hold on to me forever, to keep me for his own. But I felt the weight of all those eyes, and the great eye of Sabrael Himself.

The Patrons clapped louder than they had for any other boy. The sound was bitter in my ears, as if they'd thrown black ashes on us. Romejin must have seen the anger flash in my eyes. He wrapped his arms around me, thrust himself deep into me again and again, until I could think of nothing but the feel of every inch of him filling me. Breathing hard, I kissed his sculpted chest, brushed my fingertips over his face.

He started a subtle rocking motion that made my own cock throb and jerk between us. I didn't want it to end. I wanted to go on being his until the brightest stars in every galaxy burned to dim memories of light. He held me down on him, thrust harder and faster.

"Master." My breath came in short gasps. "I didn't know

it would be like this." I looked into his straining face. "Don't let them—" He pulled me down on his cock with a strength I'd never felt and thrust savagely into me.

I threw my head back, cried out.

Romejin came inside me, bucking, grunting, filling my ass with hot cum. The Patrons surged to their feet, polite applause drowned in their roar of approval. He lifted me, rose to his feet, held me against him. "I will take him to bathe," he said, "so that he will be clean for your pleasure."

The Patrons, pleased at his performance, murmured their agreement.

Romejin spun me around to face him, his arms rigid around me. "I'm a Believer," he said. "Hold on."

I squeezed him even closer to me and then we were falling, holding each other.

The section of floor beneath us had become a Chute, but steeper than any I'd ever known. We zoomed down into the depths of the ship.

Sabrael's voice boomed all around us. "Where are you taking the boy?"

I landed on top of Romejin, our naked bodies tangled together. He rolled to his feet, pulled me up. "Run."

"Why do you play this foolish game?" Sabrael said. "He belongs to me."

"Faster," Romejin said between breaths.

"There is nowhere for you to go," Sabrael said. His voice thundered loud enough to hurt my ears. "I am your world."

Ahead the walls faded from red to pink to—nothing. Not a ray of light escaped the throat of night.

I stopped short. "The dark." Every breath was a small agony. "We can't. We'll die." Romejin pressed me against the wall, kissed me hard.

"Will you let that be the last time I touch you?" The thought
of losing him was unbearable.

"But no one survives the dark," I said.

Romejin drove his fist into the wall behind me.

"Sabrael has gone insane. He will journey through space
forever, breeding us like animals."

I took his fist in my trembling hands, pulled his fingers to my
lips.

"We can go back. Beg forgiveness."

In a moment, he'd taken both my wrists in one strong hand.

"In the dark," he said, "we will be free of him."

I pulled away, slipped my fingers through his.

Together, we stepped out of Sabrael's eternal day, and slipped
into darkness so complete that for the first time in my life, my
world was without walls.

Icy cold wind rushed past us. Sabrael had opened part of
himself. In seconds, we would be sucked into the freezing sea of
deep space. Hands came out of the dark and grabbed me, threw
me to the floor. I heard Romejin crash down beside me. A door
slammed shut. The wind stopped. Brilliant light flooded into the
world.

"Are you well?" a man said. "We had to—"

A harsh voice interrupted. "Never mind them. Launch. Now.
Before the gate closes."

We seemed to be alone after that. Romejin stood, pulled me
into his arms, whispered, "Be brave a little longer, Tesh."

I felt the sting of a needle sliding into my neck.

The dark truly came for me. The Unbearable Torment had
found me and I could not outrun it; could only sink down into
it, deeper than I had ever known.

* * *

Shards of memory floated through my mind.

The cool feel of a platform underneath me.

Romejin's warmth beside me.

His hand in mine.

Glass rising up, sealing us in.

Falling.

His words came back, *I'm a Believer.*

We'd fallen through space on a Life Boat. But to where?

I opened my eyes and saw dark shadows on a strange starless sky. A white stick stood on a stone near me. Light wavered above it, a strange light that rose and fell as though it breathed.

A part of the wall opened, then Romejin was beside me. His hands roamed my body, finding places that were tender. I winced, but made no move to stop him.

"I didn't know you were awake," he said.

"Where are we?"

"We're free. Sabrael can't control our lives anymore."

I heard the low sounds of other men. We were inside something. When I asked, Romejin said it was called a tent. "Won't we die, without Sabrael to watch over us?"

"We'll live as our forefathers intended, not as slaves to a metal god gone mad."

I brushed my hand over his solid body.

"You're still my Master?" I said.

He kissed me, explored every inch of my body as if for the first time. "Say my name," he said. "Since I first saw you, I've longed to hear my name on your lips."

I was living a Forbidden Tale, dreaming a dangerous dream.

"I want to be yours, Romejin, forever."

"For as long as you desire," he said.

And then, I held him tight.

TINTED WINDOWS

Shane Allison

James can't suck dick for shit. His lips feel nice enough, but he doesn't apply any pressure. "Don't nut in my mouth," he said. Considering how many times he frequents the arcade, he oughta be gargling cum like it's mouthwash. Everybody knows he's a glory-hole slut. But man, the way he hums on a dick, his gay membership card should be suspended until he learns how to properly give oral sex.

Cynthia, who works until midnight, has closed the arcade off with box tape and a sign that reads, CLOSED FOR CLEANING, THANKS, X-MART. All they do is sweep and mop the floors. Men go back there and do some of the nastiest shit, like using the booth as a toilet, or spitting cum in the corners after they've blown some breeder. Hell, I went in and saw that someone had smeared shit across the walls. Just last week I sat in somebody's pee, probably was some jealous queen who couldn't stand the fact that I was getting all the hot college dick, like it's my fault they think I give good head.

I decide against a movie this weekend considering I only have nine bucks to my name, which I have to split for gas and food. I pump three bucks into the tank of my Mama's Taurus SE and finally decide on chicken and biscuits for dinner. I drive to Seminole Bowl where Chris works—this cute, big dick of a boy I have a crush on. He'll be getting off in the next hour or so. They've already started disconnecting the neon beer signs. I see he's driving his own car tonight. Glad to know that Clara, his chicken-head of a girlfriend, won't be picking him up.

I can smell the fumes from the fresh gas I've just pumped. The chicken is well seasoned and off the hook. Kanye West seeps through the cylindrical speakers. If I have to hear "Gold Digger" one more time, I'm gonna drive to 107.1 radio station and rip D.J. Demp's gold grill out of his mouth. I know this song forward and backward. I was gonna buy his new album since I didn't get *College Dropout,* but he's become so commercialized, I might just skip this one too.

I can't hear the concert going on next door at AJ's due to the group of rowdy sista girls hanging out in front of Dollar General. Why they gotta be so loud, and where in the hell did they get those Gloria Gaynor disco purses? I know the '70s ain't makin' a comeback, 'cause I'll be damned if I'm gonna wear platform boots and bell-bottoms. I already have the Afro but only because I'm too lazy to go to the barbershop.

Chris says I can come over tonight. He says that Clara's out of town for a family reunion or some shit. Good thing, 'cause after I'm done eatin', I'll be ready for some dessert. Chris with whipped cream around his balls and a cherry on his dick will make for a tasty after-dinner treat. I told him on the phone that when I'm done with him, there'll be nothing left. There goes the Budweiser light, then Michelob, Miller's, Coors. Because two people didn't show up for work, he had to open and close. I'm sure he's past ready to go. He better have some energy for me, I know that.

As I suck the last chunks of meat from the chicken thigh, I nearly choke on it when I see what's goin' down. I drop the greasy meat into the box that rests in my lap to rub the early morning sleep out of my eyes just to make sure I wasn't seeing things. A bald, brown-skinned beefcake is standing in the open door of a smoke-gray jeep massaging his dick. He smiles and nods his head as if he's talking to someone in the driver's seat. All I can see are Reeboks attached to a set of sweatpant legs. The guy looks around to see if everything is cool before he forks out his dick over the elastic of blue jogging pants. Fuck, he's huge! I'm shocked that they would take such a risk especially with the sheriff's car parked in front of the bowling alley. The X-rated scene is better than any porn video as I watch the guy inside the car devour this fine-ass brotha's dick in the parking lot. He nervously continues to look around to make sure no one's coming. He looks directly at me, but he can't see past the tint that shades my windshield. I envy the dude sucking his dick. Lucky motherfucker!

It's not long before my own dick is hard, stretching within its tomb of white draws. I take a bottle of poppers out of my pocket and take a deep whiff. Jacking off in the car is uncomfortable, there's no room to stretch. I left the lube in my backpack at the house, but my hands are good and greasy from the fried chicken, so it will have to do. The muscle-bound stranger tucks his dick back into the warm security of his jogging pants when he hears the faint sounds of conversation and cars turning into the shopping outlet of the Dollar General.

"Coast is clear, baby," I say, whispering in the midst of fast-food fried chicken and *Vanillaroma* car fresheners. The guy resumes sucking the brute's dick as I lean into the plush seat to unfasten my jeans. I fish out my hard-on with greasy fingers, smear precum over a chestnut-brown, bulbous dickhead. I can only make out the profile of his face being churned by this guy's crazy inches. I don't take my eyes off his dick; I'm wishing I was the set of lips around it, wishing it was my spit dripping off his hefty ball sac. With greasy fingers, it's hard to get a firm grip on my dick. Jacking off is nearly impossible with the steering wheel practically cradled in my lap. Surprisingly, the chicken grease works better than any bottle of lotion or cheap sex store lubricant. This guy's been at it, according to the digital clock on my stereo, a good half an hour, and surprisingly, neither they nor I have been spotted in our acts of lewdness and indecency beneath these Saturday night stars. As the guy inside the car deep-throats the one standing and fucking his mouth with nothing but tinted glass to cloak them, I think the guy getting blown must be close to coming by now. I forget the bigger the dick, the longer it takes to get off. I want us to come together. I draw close to climax. I pull the elastic of my draws around a set of tender balls. The windows are fogged over. My mama's car reeks of poppers and chicken. I've spent all day saving myself for Chris, but this can't wait. It won't. I watch them as I beat off in an amyl nitrate haze.

"Suck it," I whisper. "Suck that dick!" I can feel the cool, fall air blow across my sweaty face as cars zoom down the street of the Tennessee Street strip.

My muscles tighten and tense when cum explodes onto the steering wheel, oozing over greasy fingers. Blood rushes to my brain as sweat burns my eyes. I make out the man, who looks like a black Kojak, through a windshield riddled with specs of dirt and bird crap, and the guy sucking him with relentless fever. The cars and college-aged club junkies are but a blur. His legs tremor against the cocksucker's lips. I massage my balls as he uncorks his dick from a talented mouth. He coaxes his wet dick over the other guy and comes between his legs on cracked, sun-bleached asphalt.

It's 2:09 and the last few neon lights have been shut off. The one guy tucks his legs back into the car while the standing guy and I tuck ourselves back into our pants. I want to flash my headlights to let them know I have been watching all along, but I figure not knowing that they've been watched is all the charm. Chris and the sheriff head out into a night cloaked with early morning dew. The standing guy bends to put his arms on the burly shoulders of his man, smothering him with kisses.

Chris makes his way toward my car carrying his backpack.

"Hey, babe," I say.

"Hey."

"You won't believe what I saw."

"What up?" he asks as he sets his pack in the backseat.

"I'll tell you on the way."

I crank the car and drive off toward his place.

GOD'S OWN EXHIBITIONIST

Simon Sheppard

This all started several years back; four years ago to be precise, which means 1997.

I travel a lot. A whole lot. This time I was in India. Out on the outskirts of Delhi, there's a building called Humayun's Tomb. Kind of a precursor to the Taj Mahal, it's a big Muslim mausoleum with a colossal domed interior, imposing, maybe even a bit creepy. It's not a big tourist destination, sort of in the middle of nowhere, and one spring afternoon I found myself all alone in this huge old place. I looked up, surrounded by the past, the presence of death, of history and...well, I just got horny, intensely horny. I peered out of a doorway, across the garden—nobody coming.

I unzipped my pants and pulled out my cock, which was already half-hard. I was showing myself to nobody. Therefore, I was showing myself to everybody, even to the whole universe, and if that doesn't make much sense, it nevertheless made me happy. And harder.

Now, I'm sure if some mullah somewhere found out about what I did, he'd get righteously pissed off, so let me say right here that no sacrilege was intended. And even if it had been, hey, I'm an equal-opportunity offender; when I was a grad student at Berkeley, I got fucked in a church pew...though it *was* a Unitarian Church, so maybe that doesn't count.

Anyway, I stood there in the immensity of the place and beat off, no sound but the cawing of ravens in the warm distance. It didn't take me long. Beneath a dome nearly vast as the heavens it was standing in for, staring up into the architectural void, I jacked off—my muscles tightened, hips thrust forward—and I had one of the most intense orgasms of my life, big spurts of jizz spewing across the geometries of the inlaid floor, shattering the order of a perfectly arranged cosmos. I licked my hand clean, stuffed my dick back in my pants and took a few snapshots.

It was like I'd just fucked infinity.

The next time I did something like that, it was somewhere very far from Delhi in the spring. I was in Saint Louis in the middle of a pelting rainstorm, driving a friend's old Ford Festiva cross-country—don't ask—when the car broke down in the caffeinated middle of the night, on a deserted street right near the Gateway Arch. It was pissing down rain, blurring the sharp steel profile of the floodlit parabola. I'd never been to Saint Louis before, in fact, had never been to Missouri, and I had no idea of what I was going to do, not at 3:00 A.M. I was flummoxed. And I was, decisively, horny. At first I sat there in the misbehaving car, the still-alive radio blaring out some banal '80s oldie, my hand working my dick through my jeans. Then I figured *What the hell?* and pulled out my cock. Staring up at Saarinen's great, meaningless curve, I wondered if I was somehow queer for arches and domes, a parabola fetishist. Whatever. I got out of the Ford, my hard, slightly curved, and, if I do say so myself, impressive dick throbbing.

I stood facing the car, so that if any other damp, unfortunate soul happened by, he'd probably mistake me for a drunk taking a piss. I stared upward to the crest of the immense arch. Cold rain soaking most all of me, I gripped down hard on my dick, squeezing and pulling at it, forcing it and the rest of me farther and farther away from Saint Louis and closer and closer toward the point of no return. My eyes lost focus, my mouth filled with rain, and my sperm, one more liquid amidst the storm, flew in mini-arcs onto the white Festiva, where it was washed, presumably, into the gutter, maybe to eventually join the timeless flow of the mighty Mississippi. Or else headed, who knows, to some purification plant, perhaps winding up in the drinking glass of some adamant Midwestern Republican.

My parabola-equals-lust theory was put to the test some six months later in Paris, when I'd finally dried out from that night in Saint Louis. I got up just before dawn and made my way to the *Place du Trocadéro*, just across the Seine from one of the greatest phallic erections of modern man, the Eiffel Tower. I was gratified to note that my dick responded equally well to another sort of architecture. There wasn't a *gendarme* in sight. With the help of my camera's auto-timer, I was able to document myself shooting my nut in front of Monsieur Eiffel's masterwork, a cliché pointed heavenward.

Now there was no stopping me. I managed to engage in a session of monumental self-abuse wherever I went. In front of the Colossi of Memnon in Egypt's Valley of the Kings. Down in the dungeon of a Crusaders' castle, in Syria of all places. A good deal less improbably, at the Vatican. At Machu Picchu, while being watched impassively by lamas. Coming back from an orgasmic stroll across the Golden Gate Bridge, I beat off again in the near-empty last car of a late-night subway train, though

the thrill was squelched when I realized that two other guys in
the car were doing exactly the same thing.

And I documented each sneaky cumshot with a self-timed
photo, which I then put up on a website that began getting an
inordinate number of hits. It's not like I'm a total show-off, but
I did like the fact that somewhere out there, another man, all
alone, was jacking off to an image of me jacking off. Sometimes
just thinking about that made me want to masturbate myself, so
I did. Somebody even started a jealous rumor that the shots were
Photoshopped fakes. They're not, of course. I just happen to
have a job that takes me all over the world, a bunch of frequent-
flyer miles—and a hyperactive libido.

And then I got to New York. To celebrate the freedom of the
flesh, I figured a pilgrimage to Lady Liberty was in order. I got
up bright and early, before the late-August heat hit, and headed
down to the tip of Manhattan, catching the very first boat to
Liberty Island. When the ferry docked, I sprinted, despite the
admonitions of the Park Police, to the statue's entrance and
was the first visitor to arrive at the gate. A backpack check—
no bomb—was followed by an elevator ride part-way, then the
climb up the endless, queasily spiraling stairs that lead to the
crown of the Lady with the Torch. I'd been in training for a
marathon, so I fairly flew up the staircase, upward through the
innards of the narrowing torso, all the way to the top. I'd left all
the other tourists far behind me, their fading footsteps almost
inaudible. I had a few precious minutes all to myself. After
barely glancing through the surprisingly small windows toward
the skyline of Manhattan—the deco beauty of the Chrysler
Building, the overbearing slabs of the World Trade Center—I
found a place to set up my camera, pushed the self-timer button,
spit in my hand, and, calf muscles screaming, got down to work.
I stroked my anxious hard-on for all its pleasure-soaked nerves

were worth, but it looked like I wouldn't, damn it, have time to unleash my huddled spermatozoa yearning to breathe free. Tourists' multilingual voices were coming steadily closer. And closer still. The camera clicked, and I managed to put away my cock just moments before two fairly homely Middle Eastern guys in their twenties struggled up the final flight of stairs. I'd worn a loose jacket to cover the evidence, and so, as the small space in the crown quickly grew more crowded, I headed back down. Mission accomplished. Or almost accomplished, short an emission of sperm.

I was in the statue's museum, next to a fetishistic mockup of the Lady's gigantic sandal-clad foot, when it happened. Three uniformed National Park Police came up to me, and asked me to "Come this way, please, sir."

Okay, how the hell was I to know that the statue's insides were under constant video surveillance? Paranoid fucks. Listen, it's not like I'm some Third World terrorist bent on bombing the Statue of Liberty into copper smithereens. It's not even like they said it was, that I committed an obscene act. I mean, I'm an artist, and jacking off is part of my art, a vital part, and what the fuck's "obscenity," anyway?

I guess they expected me to plead guilty and skulk off, but listen, it's been centuries since the Puritans landed here, bringing their damn uptight ways with them, and enough is enough. This is America, right? Land of the free? 2001? We're not afraid of dick, our *enemies* are afraid of dick. So I told them I wanted a lawyer, which is why you're here, and I know maybe you think it's weird, my reaching under the table like this, but I think you and I both know what I'm up to down there, and now there's just one thing I want to know.

Do you think you can get me off?

MUSCLED SHOWER SHOW

Wayne Mansfield

I knew my public swimming pool very well. I swam there five nights a week. Lap after lap I'd slog it out until I'd done three kilometers. It had taken me a year to build up to that distance, and now that I had reached my goal I was concentrating on getting my time down.

I was getting annoyed with the amount of traffic in the lanes, but this being a public swimming pool there was nothing I could do about it. I'd be trying to beat my time and someone quite obviously in the wrong lane would be plodding along in front of me. Oftentimes I could swim around them, bypassing the offender and shooting him a dirty look as I sucked in another mouthful of air, but that didn't help me and my quest to improve my speed.

Through necessity I started going later and later until I was swimming in a nearly empty pool, immediately before the complex closed. Some nights were better than others, but one night in particular will always stick in my mind.

I'd been held up at work. It was dark when I left, but I had my swimsuit in my briefcase so I was able to go straight to the pool. There was something kind of eerie about the pool that night. It seemed completely deserted. I put that down to the oncoming autumn and the accompanying lower temperatures. Nevertheless, I was thrilled to find only one other lane occupied.

Without wasting any time I dived in, the cool water instantly washing the day's stresses away. I began swimming freestyle, pacing myself so I didn't get worn out. After fifteen laps of freestyle, I did fifteen of backstroke and then fifteen of breaststroke. Butterfly was a bit too much for my capabilities, and as I wasn't training for an Olympic marathon I didn't feel guilty about not including it in my fitness regimen. I finished up with quite a few more laps of freestyle.

By the time I pulled myself up out of the water and onto the side of the pool I was alone. I walked across the cool concrete, across a small patch of grass and up the stairs to the changing rooms. Even from the doorway I could hear one of the showers going. They were communal showers, two rows of ten showerheads facing each other in a tiled area, hidden by a wall that separated it from the toilet block.

I stripped off my swimsuit, hung it on a hook by my bag and padded, naked, past the urinals and the cubicles containing the toilets and turned the corner.

The scene that confronted me stopped me in my tracks.

There were two men locked in an embrace, their lips pressed together as their hands roamed over each other's V-shaped torsos. Both had the kind of body I aspired to: Honed. Sculpted. Perfect.

I stepped back behind the wall, undetected and aroused. My heart was pounding, its beat loud in my ears. I glanced over my shoulder to check the area behind me, then returned my attention to the two men under the shower, peering like a naughty schoolboy around the corner.

One of the men was blond and had an all-over tan. He was taller and at that moment had his back to me. The other man was slightly shorter, broad shouldered and hairy. His chest hair was thick, luxuriant and the very sight of it made my rock-hard cock twitch. He was deeply tanned except where his swimsuit had been, the whiteness accentuating the perfect orb of the one buttcheek I could see.

As the blond guy dropped to his knees, my hand dropped to my throbbing cock, which by now was dribbling thick ropes of precum. My heart was still going a mile a minute. This was excitement and danger, both in equal measure. I kept looking over my shoulder, checking for pool staff, and then returning my attention to the hot cocksucking action happening right in front of me.

Mr. Dark had a massive pole on him, thick and heavily veined, the deep pink cockhead glistening with Mr. Blond's spit. I almost began to salivate as I watched Mr. Blond open his throat and swallow the mighty rod all the way down to the pubes and back again. His mouth caressed the swollen shaft as he pulled his head back, and when the engorged cockhead reached his lips, he sucked it firmly before pushing his head forward again, taking the entire length once again down his throat.

I was getting a front-seat, side-on view, and they hadn't even noticed me. That made the whole situation electric, hot enough to force me to take my hand off my cock in case I shot my load too soon.

Mr. Dark kept glancing in my direction, no doubt checking to see if the coast was clear. I was worried that he might catch me spying, get nervous and bring the whole show to an end. I did my best to stay out of sight, but it didn't take long for the inevitable to happen.

I was seen.

My heart began to slam against my rib cage. I hid from view, too late, and wondered what the hell I was going to do. Should I sneak back to the changing area? Perhaps do a few more laps then come in again? None of that was going to happen. My curiosity was too overpowering. I took a deep breath and peered once again around the corner.

Mr. Dark was still looking in my direction, but surprisingly, he was smiling. He gave me a wink and put a finger up to his mouth to indicate silence. My cock, which had started to deflate, sprang back to attention. Now that one of them knew I was there, getting off on watching them, I was more turned on than if I had been over there with them.

Mr. Dark turned around and leaned against the tiled wall. He reached around and pulled his meaty buttcheeks apart, exposing the thickly-haired crack to Mr. Blond, who wasted no time in plunging his tongue into the furry abyss.

With his right hand busy between his own legs, tugging frantically on another large piece of meat, Mr. Blond sucked and slurped at Mr. Dark's pucker like a wild animal. His face disappeared for whole minutes at a time, too busy tongue-fucking the tasty pucker to come up for air.

Mr. Dark's head fell back against his shoulders and a small moan escaped his lips. He thrust his arse farther out and took a firmer grip on each cheek, pulling them as far apart as he could. He started grinding his hairy arsehole against Mr. Blond's face before one massive paw of a hand reached back, grabbed the squatting man's head and pulled it deeper into his crack.

Mr. Blond pulled back, gasped for air and then allowed himself to be forced back into Mr. Dark's furry crevice, lips parted and tongue ready.

I was now fingering my hole, wanting more than anything to have something more substantial up there. I arched my back, pushing down onto my finger and slipping a second digit inside. I closed my eyes for a moment to enjoy the sensation. Then, while I leaned against the wall with my shoulder, my free hand returned to my cock—and my eyes returned to the fuck session.

Mr. Blond was standing up. His cock was rigid, almost parallel to his smooth, washboard stomach. He pushed it down and let it spring back up to slap against his belly. I heard it from where I stood.

I pushed my two fingers deeper into my hole and moaned quietly to myself. I ached for Mr. Blond's steel-hard organ to penetrate and invade me. I wanted both their cocks inside me, one after the other, or together, at the same time. I wanted more than anything to walk over there and join them, but I wasn't sure if they'd let me. So I waited.

Mr. Blond reached over Mr. Dark's shoulder and pressed the handle down on the soap dispenser half a dozen times. Slowly, he smeared the liquid soap over his throbbing cock while his lips left a trail of tiny kisses over Mr. Dark's back. When his cock was covered in foamy bubbles, he reached down and pulled one of Mr. Dark's arsecheeks open. With his lips still on Mr. Dark's back he guided his cock into Mr. Dark's hole. I heard another moan: was it his or mine?

Mr. Dark's hands found his nipples. His stout fingers twisted the fleshy nubs this way and that before the pressure of Mr. Blond's gentle thrusts had him bracing himself against the wall.

Mr. Blond looked over in my direction. I wasn't sure whether he had seen me, but as their fucking grew in intensity they were both looking in my direction more and more. Their nervousness was catching. I found myself getting spooked at every little noise. It must have been getting close to closing time, but it was a big complex so I had to take a chance that whatever the staff had to do in the changing rooms, they would do later.

It didn't take long for Mr. Blond to begin pounding Mr. Dark. There wasn't a lot of time to take things slowly. Someone could walk in at any moment.

"I'm gonna come," said Mr. Blond, panting.

With those magic words I felt my own balls tightening. I kept my hand firmly wrapped around my cock and my two fingers buried as far inside me as I could push them. My eyes stayed riveted to the couple under the showers.

Mr. Blond's arse muscles were mesmerizing as they contracted and expanded under his taut skin.

"Ahh, here it comes," Mr. Blond grunted. "I'm gonna shoot!"

At that moment I stepped out into the shower room, exposing myself. My fingers were still inside me, and my hand was jerking my cock. Both men looked at me. Mr. Dark smiled. Mr. Blond looked a bit shocked, but he was beyond the point of no return. I had chosen my time well. Mr. Blond's eyes stayed on my cock for a few seconds, taking in the vision of me standing there, jerking off and riding my fingers. Then he closed his eyes and thrust upward, keeping his cock deep inside Mr. Dark's arsehole as he blew his load. He thrust again, as a second or third jet of creamy man-paste erupted into Mr. Dark's tight, hairy fuck-hole.

I couldn't hold off anymore. I grunted, drawing both men's attention. A thick, pearly white stream of warm cum erupted from the head of my cock, arcing through the air and splattering across the beige tiles of the shower area. I thrust my hips upward as a second, third and fourth jet rocketed out, splashing against the tiles.

"Thanks, guys," I said, flicking a bead of sperm from my hand.

Mr. Blond nodded and slowly pulled his glistening cock out of Mr. Dark.

"Not over yet," said Mr. Dark. "I still haven't unloaded."

I twisted the taps to the nearest shower on, but when I turned back around Mr. Dark was standing right in front of me.

"Didn't you hear me, mate," he said. "I've got a two-day load to get rid of."

Suddenly he had me around the waist. His hands were large and strong. He picked me up and threw me over his shoulder; putting my face directly against his furry arsecheek. As he carried me across to where he and Mr. Blond had been fucking, I could see a thin, faint dribble of cum running down his leg.

He hoisted me off his shoulder, and I landed roughly on my feet, grabbing hold of him to stop myself from falling over. With barely enough time for me to get my balance he had me up against the wall.

"Now you get your chance to be the main attraction," he said, his voice deep and commanding. "You mind keeping an eye out, buddy? I won't be long."

Mr. Blond nodded and moved back to the last showerhead, which gave him a view of the short corridor that led into the shower area. Mr. Dark pumped the handle of the soap dispenser and wiped the accumulated liquid soap on his cock.

"You should be nice and loose by now," he said. "How many fingers did you have up there?"

I didn't answer. I had seen how thick his cock was, and I was bracing myself for penetration. Outside I could hear the sounds of the pool staff cleaning up. My heart was racing, again. My breathing had become rapid and shallow. I kept looking at Mr. Blond for any indication that someone was coming.

Mr. Dark slipped his hairy middle finger into my arse.

"Nice and tight," he said. "Beautiful."

The next thing I knew I felt the head of his cock pushing against my sphincter. I arched my back, pushing my arsehole onto his cock. I winced as it pushed past the tight ring of muscle and then inhaled, long and slow, as he pushed his prong deep inside me.

It felt better than I had expected. The rim of my hole was stretched tight around his cock, and I could feel his huge organ filling me.

He reached around with one hand and pinched one of my nipples. With the other, he played with my semihard cock. I felt totally dominated, exposed. This man had me in his grip. I was impaled on his large cock. I couldn't escape even if I wanted to, which I didn't. As he began to thrust, as I felt his warm breath on the back of my neck, I felt myself getting hard again, despite the fact I had only blown a load not two minutes ago.

"How's my big cock feel inside you?" he asked. "You're loving it, aren't you?"

I nodded. I couldn't do anything else. I was a prisoner, not only of him but of my desires. I'd had no intention of becoming part of this public fuck, but now that I was, I was going to enjoy it.

I looked at Mr. Blond, who was washing himself under the shower.

Strange, I thought. *If I was him, I'd be watching me and Mr. Dark.* A light frown appeared on my face.

I focused my attention on the beige tiles in front of me and on the warm sensation centered on my arsehole but rapidly spreading throughout my body. I had never felt so invaded, or so excited. My stiff cock was a testament to my enjoyment. I reached down and took it in my hand. It felt good to stroke it even though my chances of blowing another load were slim.

Mr. Dark gripped my hips and began to grind against my buttcheeks. His cock was so far inside me that I could feel his wet pubic hair scratching against the tender white skin of my butt. It didn't take long for his thrusts to get faster and harder. His grip tightened; his hands pulled me back against him violently, urgently. My whole body was being shaken.

"I'm getting close, boy," he said, his voice barely audible above our puffing and panting. I looked again at Mr. Blond, who was now drying himself. Again I had the fleeting thought that it was strange he wasn't paying any attention to us. Then I caught him looking up toward the corridor and then at me. I looked over my shoulder and saw one of the pool attendants standing there with one hand on his hip and the other rubbing against the front of his shorts.

My eyes became as wide as dinner plates as I looked away. I swallowed hard.

Mr. Dark was ramming his cock into me now. The slapping sound of our wet, naked bodies fucking filled the shower room. It was all I could hear, even though Mr. Dark's mouth was right by my ear, groaning.

"I'm gonna come," he said. "Gonna cream your tight hole."

My hand began moving faster on my cock. There was a small chance I was going to blow again. Mr. Dark's cock was giving my prostate a serious massage, and the pool attendant now had his cock out from under the bottom of his shorts and was stroking it. Mr. Blond had disappeared.

"Here I go," said Mr. Dark. "Fuck, mate. I'm gonna come."

He slammed into me, unleashing a torrent of ball juice into my greedy hole. I felt the first surge hit the soft tissue of my bowels, then nothing except Mr. Dark trying to get farther into me as he emptied his balls. Then, after he had finished and pulled himself out, I heard the voice of the pool attendant.

"I should report you guys," he said, pushing Mr. Dark out of the way as he kneeled behind me.

Then I felt the tickle of the pool attendant's mustache on my arsehole and the firmness of his tongue pushing into it. He sucked and slurped at my hole like a rabid animal, but I wasn't going to say anything. I didn't want to be banned from the pool. This guy could do whatever the hell he wanted to. He rimmed my well-fucked hole while his hand worked his hard cock. I pushed back to give him a more thorough experience, and as I did I heard him grunt. I looked down and saw a gush of thick white cum shoot across the tiles between my legs. I smiled.

"Now you guys better get dressed and get out of here. I've got to clean this mess up," he said, licking his lips. "And don't let me catch you doing anything like that again."

Mr. Dark winked at me. There was a twinkle in his eye that I will never forget. But after he turned the corner, I never saw him again. And I never again experienced anything as wild as I did that night at the public pool.

GOOD BOY

Jeff Mann

Jon always paces when he's on the phone with his wife. His deep voice veers into small and tight. He almost sounds afraid. We have little time tonight, as usual, and I'm far from a patient man, but I don't want to add to his anxiety. I don't seize the phone and throw it across the room. I don't punch him in the jaw, tear off his clothes, cuff him and shove him belly down onto the cot in the corner. Instead, I sit wearily back in the desk chair, feigning nonchalance, sipping the flask of bourbon he hoards for my rare visits. I keep my hungry hands to myself.

The rear office of Spartan Sporting Goods is cluttered, as usual. Boxes of athletic equipment line the shelves; invoices are scattered across the desktop. The only light's a lamp turned low. Despite the humming space heater, it's chilly. Cold emanates from the curtained window over the desk. February's whistling around the building.

"Later, honey," says Jon, closing his cell phone with an irri-table click, slipping it into his pocket. With a big sigh, he drops to his knees before me—the position I most savor him in. He kisses the tops of my Carhartt work boots, then wraps his big arms tightly around my waist and rests his head in my lap.

"Sorry, Sir. I know you hate to wait. I told her I was doing inventory. We have about two hours." His voice is back to normal now, the soft bass rumble I love. He nuzzles the hard lump in my jeans.

"Good boy," I say, laying one hand on his shoulder. His hard-muscled warmth is such a relief. Lately it feels like winter's soughing inside me, heaping up snowdrifts in my guts. "Front door locked?"

"Yes, Sir. And the CLOSED sign hung up. Still snowing out?"

"Yep," I say, stroking the short black hair of his buzz cut. "The parking lot's all white. In fact, the roads are getting icy. Might be you could call in a bit and tell her you'd better spend the night here. You have some blankets, right?"

Jon chuckles. "Yes, Sir. The cot's mighty narrow, though. You'll have to hold me close."

"No problem there." We so rarely get to spend a night together. Almost always, all we can manage are furtive quickies after store hours. To hold him all night will be sheer paradise. I'd like to tell him that, but I don't. I feel vulnerable enough. Both of us feel vulnerable, I think, afraid to admit feeling, afraid to admit we're more than fuckbuddies now.

I cup Jon's chin, lifting his face to mine. His brows are raven wings, his black eyelashes absurdly long, his eyes forest green. I rub a thumb over the faint shadows of his sideburns and goatee. How young guys manage to maintain that slight bit of beard I don't know—it looks like sculpted, perpetual three-day stubble—but it surely is hot. It's Jon's compromise, I think: his wife hates facial hair, I dote on it. I brush my own beard, bushy and graying, across his nose, and then I kiss him, softly, for a long time. Our tongues nestle together like fond animals, littermates. He groans, hands gripping my thighs. Swapped spit messes our chins.

I pull back, wiping my mouth. "Warm enough in here for you to give me a show?"

"You bet. And I have everything ready." He nods toward the gym bag by my chair. "Just as you ordered."

I rummage. Pulling out the items, I arrange them on the desk in the order I'll need them.

"Good. It's all here. Get to it then." I give him a gentle push, then lean back, propping a boot across a knee. "Strip for Daddy."

Jon peels his navy blue polo shirt over his head, toes off his loafers and shucks off his khaki pants. He stands before me, naked save for white athletic socks and a jockstrap already swollen with arousal. There's the flash of a bashful grin, then he clasps his hands behind his back, the parade rest position he knows I relish.

"Oh, damn," I sigh, taking in the sight. "Here's to you, pup." I take another flask-sip. "Stand there for a minute and let me study you."

If it weren't for the fact that he's married, he'd be the perfect cub, the perfect butch bottom: five foot nine, muscular, compact, naturally submissive, and aching for an older, larger, stronger man to care for him and tell him what to do. Big shoulders, big arms, big chest—the boy's vain enough to keep his weight lifting up—and a small waist only lately, in his midtwenties, beginning to show some padding, now that his wrestling days are over and he's taken a sedentary job selling sporting goods. The sturdy curves of his chest and belly are matted with ink-black hair, hair that looks even darker curling against his skin's midwinter white. The same coarse animal pelt coats his forearms and legs and curls over the top and sides of his jock.

"Too cold? Those sweet little nips of yours are standing up like top hats." I lick my lips, wanting them between my teeth.

"I'm fine, Sir." Jon runs a hand through his chest hair, rubs both nipples, then returns to parade rest.

"I can't believe she wants you to shave your chest and belly."

Jon, snickering, shakes his head and rolls his eyes. "No way in hell."

"A year since we met," I say, "and you're still the hottest fucking precious puppy a man's ever had."

"Thanks, Sir, but I'm getting a little gut." Jon gifts me with another quick grin, pats his belly with mock regret and bows his head, waiting for further orders.

I laugh. "Yes, you are. And it's sexy as hell. It makes you look like less of a boy and more of a man. Collar now."

I lift the dog collar—black leather, with silver studs. Time and again, Jon's told me the only time he feels like a real man, a complete one, is when he's wearing it. Eagerly he takes it from me and buckles it about his neck.

Jon sighs. It sounds like the same rushing relief I feel every time I touch him. "Now you own me, Dad," he says with a wide white smile.

"Good boy. That's right. I own you." For a few hours, yes. Maybe overnight, if the blessed snow continues. "How about some Fetch?"

It's a simple ball of black rubber I bought in a pet store, at his request, soon after our first surreptitious meeting. Every time I hold it, I remember how lonely I was before we met, how ecstatic I was finally to discover a boy so hairy, so kinky, so ravenous for a dominating Daddy. Every time I hold it, I wish I'd met him before he married her, and I pray that one day he'll leave her.

It goes on for a good while, this simple game. I toss the ball, he romps after it on hands and knees, grips it in his mouth, brings it back to me and drops it, spit-slick, into my hand, with a happy, shamefaced smile. "Good boy," I whisper. "Sweet puppy." I pat his head before tossing it again, admiring the adorable wiggle of his bubble-butt, the fuzzy crack of his ass, the ripple of muscles in his smooth back and furry thighs as he crawls over the carpet to retrieve his prize.

By the time we're done, I'm faintly bourbon-buzzed and he's positively panting. "Boots," I say. Jon drops onto his elbows, lapping my Carhartts as if he were famished. I pat my pup's prettily propped-up butt—soon enough to be subjected to the hard pounding he's always begging for—and finger the thick hair between his cheeks. I tongue-wet my forefinger and tease the edges of his hole. He wags his butt like a dog; I lick crack-musk from my finger, then push into him just a fraction. Moaning, he bucks back onto me, lapping my boots harder. I finger-fuck him, slowly, tenderly, with shallow strokes.

"Okay, pup. More of that later. Sit."

Jon gives both boots last licks, then straightens up. I hand him the next toy.

"Gag yourself. I want a good bucket of doggie-drool."

Jon takes the Wiffle ball between his teeth, then removes it. "Sir? May I speak first?"

Why does he look so sad? I nod, mustering an impassive face. "Yes, pup, speak."

"I, uh, Sir, I know that you... I'm just so sorry." His lower lip trembles; to my surprise, a fat tear slides down his cheek. "I just can't right now. You know? Leave her? But, oh, man, I really need you, I need you *so* bad. I know you're not happy with how things are, but please don't give up on me. Please don't—"

"You're afraid of what folks in this pissant town would

think. Leaving her for another man, and one twenty years older? I know, I know. I don't want to talk about this now," I growl. My gut's a bowl of ice melt. "Strap that ball in your mouth, shut up and do what you're fucking told."

Jon obeys, taking the perforated white ball between his teeth and buckling the gag's leather straps behind his head.

"Now these." Rather than hand them to him, I drop them on the floor. I don't want him to see my hand shaking. "Don't worry. They're rubber-tipped; they won't mark you up. You can endure these for a while, right? For your Dad?"

Nodding, Jon retrieves them. He looks up at me, eyes wet. I want to kiss his pretty gagged mouth, with its shadowy, stylish goatee. I want to wipe that tear from his cheek. Instead, I say, "Go on. And get those eyes down, dammit."

My pup drops his gaze to his bare chest and applies the tweezer clamps one by one to chill-hard nipples. He winces and whimpers.

"Keep going," I say, my voice low and stern. He slides the tiny rings tighter; the clamp teeth bite deeper.

Jon groans. Inside his jock, his cock bounces.

"Tighter."

Another groan. Another jock-sheathed bounce.

"All the way," I say, sipping the flask. He obeys. A harsh gasp breaks from him. His nipples have always been so sensitive, so tender. So deliciously susceptible to torture.

"Tug the chain."

He does so. His deep groans crest and break like waves.

"Good pup. Now, here." I toss hooked lead weights on the floor. He picks them up, head still lowered.

"Both of them. Right, good boy, hang them on the chain. Now look at me."

Jon sits on his calves and lifts his head. We stare into each other's eyes. His face is crumpled, his brow agony-knit, his green eyes wet. The weights make a *V* of the clamp-chain, stretching the pink flesh of his nipples out and down. His white teeth gnash the gag. From the Wiffle ball's holes and his tautened lips, drool drips steadily.

"On your hands and knees. Good boy. Now swing the weights for me. Get a nice rhythm going."

Jon hangs his head and rocks his body. The ovals of lead move back and forth, clock pendulums ticking off the time we have left. His saliva dribbles onto the carpet, making glistening puddles in the lamplight.

"Is this what you wanted?" I stroke the sweat off his temples, catch slobber stringing from his chin and smear it on my beard.

Jon nods. His nakedness moves like tree boughs in storm. The weights tug his pec-flesh into pained and hairy cones.

"I'd really like to beat you with my belt," I say, fondling an asscheek. "You'd like that, wouldn't you?"

Jon's head bobs eagerly.

"But I can't leave any bruises, right?"

More head-bobbing: regretful.

"Go ahead and cry, pup," I sigh, propping a foot on his back. "Let loose. I think you need to."

Jon needs no further encouragement. His broken sobs flood the room. I sit there, listening to his sorrow and the wind's whistling impatience. While he cries, he continues his rocking; the weights dangle from his chest mounds, swaying like a metronome. Every now and then, I pat his head; he rubs his moist face on the back of my hand. He weeps for a good ten minutes before the tears grade off into snuffles, deep gulps, then silence.

"Brave boy. Time for your reward," I say, lifting my boot's weight from his back. "Sit up. Ease 'em off. Easy, easy."

Right one. "HuuuHHHh!" Left one. "HuuuuHHHH!"

Clamps always hurt the worst coming off.

"Come here, boy. Take a break."

Jon slumps across my knees, trembling. Reaching under him, I massage the tormented little nubs; I clasp the fullness of his pecs and squeeze them. "If you stay here tonight, I'll suckle these little honeys till dawn. Would you like that?"

"Umm-hmmmm!" Jon murmurs.

"Here you go," I say, handing him the next toy. "Up on the cot. Get the jock and socks off."

Entirely naked now, Jon leans back against the wall, legs drawn up on the cot, facing me, so I can see him lube up his asshole, finger himself, then, inch by inch, push the thick dildo inside. Gasping, he pinches a nipple, closes his eyes, slides the dildo in and out.

"That's right. A nice slow fuck. Doesn't that feel good?" I have my own cock out now, jacking it. Can't imagine anything more beautiful, a hairy-muscled, gagged boy fucking himself. "Good boy. Ride it. Work your dick now. I give you my permission. Come for me."

Jon, panting, pounds his hole with the dildo, pounds his fist with his thick pink cock. In less than a minute, he's shouting and shooting, a great arc of snowy semen that spatters my boot.

"About six feet, I'd say. That didn't take long. Guess you were due." I chuckle, wiping up the cum and licking it from my fingers. "As for this," I say, pushing my hard-on back in my pants and zipping up, "I'm saving this load for your asshole."

I open the window curtain a crack. To my delight, the world's erased. Snow continues to drift down in streetlamp light. I close the curtain and sit on the edge of the cot. Bending, I lick post-cum dribble from Jon's belly hair and cockhead. He wraps his arms around me. I unbuckle the gag and pull the dripping Wiffle ball from his mouth. "Call her," I whisper, kissing saliva-ooze from his jaw. "The roads are too dangerous."

On the phone, his voice goes small and tight again. His lips purse, a little boy's pout. I can hear her tinny whine from here. She's petulant, I can tell, sad cow having to spend the night alone.

Jon gives me a presnuggle show with the last of the toys. He sits on the cot-edge and, as ordered, secures his ankles together with athletic tape. He centers a long strip of black Everlast handwrap over his mouth, threads it between his teeth, wraps it several times around his head, and knots it behind: the soft, easy-on-the-jaw gag he's asked for those few nights we've managed to spend together. Finally, he cuffs his hands before him before stretching out on the cot. I strip, flick off the light, and climb in beside him, pulling the blankets over us.

The space heater whirs softly. Wind persists, clawing the eaves. I lie on my back, one arm wrapped around him, fondling his faint goatee. He lies on his side, buzz cut tickling my shoulder, cuffed hands stroking my belly thatch. Tomorrow night, I'll be alone again, and he'll be in bed with her.

"We'll talk tomorrow. I promise."

"Uh-huh."

"Warm enough?"

"Uh-huh."

"Happy?"

"Uhh-*huhhhhhhh*!"

"I'm going to eat that pretty hole of yours later and then take you up the ass, long and hard, just the way you like it."

With a boyish giggle, Jon rolls over and grinds his butt against my crotch. When I reach for his cock, I find it newly stiff.

"Ready to go again? Damn, you are one eager puppy. Ah, youth." I give his shaft a few short strokes, then embrace him, spooning him from behind. "Let me get a little shut-eye first, and then I'll pound you till you're raw. Didn't get much sleep last night. Bad dreams."

Jon nods, taking my hand in his.

"I hope we get a goddamn blizzard. I hope we're stuck here for days."

"Uh-huh!" Jon kisses the back of my hand. The boxing wrap is already mouth-moist.

I say it before I think it. "I don't know how much longer I can do this, pup. It's too hard, giving you up again and again." God, how I hate the quaver in my voice. "I don't know how to live without you. I think about you all the time. There's this terrible tenderness inside me. When you're not around, I'm nigh to choking on the flood of it. I love you, pup."

Jon doesn't pull away or stiffen up. What he mumbles, what I always hoped he might one day say, I can make out despite his gag.

"I love you too, Dad."

He takes a deep breath and nestles closer. Sleep is far from us now, displaced by amazement. We lie together in the dark, listening to the wind. Again and again, I kiss the back of Jon's neck. Again and again, he squeezes my hand. With the other, I cup a pec in my palm, feeling the beat of his heart, running my fingers through the hair on his breast as if it were new spring grass or summer grain.

THE BOY
IN THE CHAIR

Christopher Pierce

The watcher knows I know he's watching me.

He seems fascinated by me, obsessed maybe. It all started when I took the blinds down in my living room so I could put up new ones and then forgot all about the new blinds when I was reminded just what a beautiful view my penthouse had of the City of Angels.

I live at Park La Jolla, a gated multicomplex community in the heart of L.A., right in front of the Tar Pits. The buildings are X-shaped, so it's easy to look out your windows right into your neighbors' condos.

Suddenly my frequent sexual activities had a new level of eroticism—the thrill of being watched! Soon after my blinds came down and I continued my living room exploits right where everyone could see them, most of my neighbors closed *their* blinds. I guess even in liberal, trendy, progressive Los Angeles gay sex isn't what most people want to watch during dinnertime.

Oh, well, I figured, their loss.

But I had one neighbor who didn't close his blinds. He became my biggest fan, watching nightly to see what I got up to after dark. I never got to see him too well, but he looked like a young guy, midtwenties probably. He would set up a chair right in front of his window and jerk off while he watched me and my conquest of the night.

But tonight is the night everything changes.

The boy I've invited over is one of my regular fuckbuddies. We met about six months ago online and have been meeting for sex ever since. Earlier today I sent him email instructions for tonight's meeting. Now I make sure my watcher is in position on the other X-bar of the complex—he's there, in his chair, watching. I wonder if he notices that I've set up a chair right in front of my window, just like he always does.

My condo's front door is opening.

Time for me to disappear into the shadows of the hallway. I hear the door close.

There is a pause, during which I imagine the boy is removing his clothing as instructed. Then he walks into view, his back to me, lovely in his nakedness. He's smaller than me, five-five or so, 120 pounds, his ass round and full as two perfect melons. He walks to the chair and sits down in it. He looks out the window and across the short expanse to my watcher's window. The two boys in their chairs, almost mirror images, stare through the panes of glass at each other.

Then quick as lightning I am behind my boy, clamping one leather-gloved hand over his mouth and wrapping my other well-muscled arm around his torso. In our reflection in the window I see his eyes go wide at the sight of me, masked and clothed all in black. He reaches behind himself, grabbing me tight with both hands, securing me to the back of the chair. Keeping my left hand clamped over his mouth, I reach between his legs. The boy lets out a helpless little sound, hardly audible through my hand, as I take hold of his cock. Already a little stiff, his dick hardens and lengthens in my hand as I start to jack him off. I watch his reflection: good—as instructed he is not closing his eyes, but staring across at the watcher, who has now begun to jerk himself to mirror us.

As I beat him off, the boy's body shudders. I put my mouth to his ear and whisper filth to him. His hands clutch at me and he breathes faster and faster through his nose. Pressing his back against the chair, the boy lifts his ass a little off the seat. He begins to whine softly, like an animal in heat. I continue to jack him until his whining becomes grunting.

It won't be long now.

Glancing across I see the watcher jerking himself, but not fast, not yet. He knows there's a part two to this performance.

The boy in my arms is squirming, writhing, desperate with pleasure. I do him faster and faster and now he's gasping—it's time. My hand grips his cock even tighter and I aim it at the window. With a cry muffled by my hand still over his mouth, the boy comes. White jets of jizz squirt out of his pulsing tool to splatter onto the window glass. I release my hold on him and the boy slumps limply in the chair.

The watcher lets go of his cock—he know this is only half-time.

I step back and strip my clothes off slowly until I am naked, except for the mask, which I leave on. I let my clothes fall to the floor.

"Get off the chair," I say to the boy.

"Yes, Sir," he whispers and slips off the chair into a kneeling position on the floor, his eyes level with his splats of spunk on the window that are still dripping lazily down the glass to the sill. I pick up two tubes of lube from the floor and toss one on the floor next to the boy.

"Get yourself ready," I say to the boy.

"Yes, Sir."

I sit down in the chair myself. My throbbing rod sticks straight up into the air. I slick it up with lube as I watch the boy massaging his own asshole with lube, preparing himself for penetration. I stare over the boy at the watcher, who has begun to masturbate again. He may not know what's next, but he knows me well enough to know that I'm not done with this boy.

When my cock and the boy's asshole are suitably lubricated I tell my guest to stand in front of me and back up a few steps. When he's within reach I grab his left hip with my left hand, then guide him down. With my right hand I aim my cock, and with smooth precision and a little help from gravity the boy impales himself perfectly on my tool. He gasps as he takes me all the way in, until his buttocks are resting on my spread inner thighs. With both hands on his hips now I lift the boy a little way up, then pull him back down, and then do it again. And again.

I tilt my head to the right and see that the watcher has resumed jacking himself, as I knew he would. I snarl in pleasure as I make the boy fuck himself with my cock. His whole body is rigid, his head rolling back to rest on my left shoulder.

We breathe in unison; lift and down, lift and down.

I'm ready to erupt. I slam the boy down one last time, and my dick fires white-hot jets of cum deep into his guts. I grit my teeth as the orgasm tears through me. I wrap both arms around the boy's torso and squeeze him so hard he gasps for air. I release him and check out the watcher.

He's lying back in his chair, his hands limp at his sides. I know he's come too.

When I've savored every last bit of pleasure from this experience, I lift the boy one last time, helping him off my cock. He tumbles onto the floor in front of me, breathing heavily. I rise from the chair, brazenly naked, and tear the mask from my face, letting it fall to the floor. There are no more barriers between us, despite glass or distance. I lean over and pick up the large handwritten sign I'd placed on the floor next to the chair earlier. I press it up against the window and watch the watcher read it:

YOU'RE NEXT and my condo number.

The watcher hesitates for just a moment, then he is up and out of his chair, grabbing for his clothes.

I look down at my guest.

He's still lying there, eyes closed, his breathing nearly slowed to normal. He's still clearly in no shape to walk, but in a minute I'm going to be entertaining a new guest, one I've been waiting to meet for a long time. I'm a considerate host: I lean over and take the boy by the wrists and lift him to his feet, then gently hoist him up and over my left shoulder. I carry him to my bedroom and lay him down in my bed. I put a pillow under his head and a blanket over his body. He sighs contentedly. I close the bedroom door behind me as I head back out to the main room.

My condo's front door is opening.

TABLE TOPPED

Cari Z

W hat, here?" Michaels exclaims, his voice a lot higher than normal.

"What's wrong with here?" I murmur in his ear as I pull him close to me again, wrapping my arms around his waist and slipping my fingertips beneath his belt.

"It's…it's Mr. Brandt's office," Michaels manages. His head is whipping from side to side, taking in everything as though he's never seen it before. Which, come to think of it, perhaps he hasn't. Matt Michaels works in accounting, has modest aspirations toward middle management, and a desk covered with pictures of his cat. I'm the vice-president of research and development for our corporation. I've been in this office plenty of times, but he's probably never had reason to before. It's likely a little intimidating. Lord knows I've found it to be so in the past.

"We can't fuck in Mr. Brandt's office, Jake," Michaels hisses. "What if someone walks in? What if *he* comes in? We'll both be fired!" Michaels and I have had the occasional interlude before in the workplace, but never in a space quite so…lofty.

"Matthew," I say evenly as I let one hand drift up to undo his tie, "it's the evening of the company holiday party. People are probably fucking everywhere right now. In the storage rooms, in the bathrooms, in the goddamn cafeteria…this is the one place we can be sure we'll be alone. Mr. Brandt has been away on business all week, and his secretary doesn't work nights. We'll be fine." I slip his tie off and let it fall to the floor, then start in on his buttons. "Unless you'd prefer waiting in line for the broom closet…"

"No," Michaels says quickly, leaning his chest into my touch even as his eyes rove over the furniture. I can tell it appeals to him. His nipples are pebble hard beneath my fingertips and his breathing is fast and shallow. He's looking at the table. Everyone looks at the table. It's a goddamn fifteen-foot, lacquered, polished-oak phallic symbol. When Henry first put it in I almost laughed myself unconscious.

I get our feet moving in the direction of that table, mindful of providing just the right view. "Do you want me to fuck you here, Matthew?" I purr, stopping my hand after the top few buttons of his shirt are undone. I want to keep some clothes between us, but I love touching his skin as well. Michaels has an incredibly smooth chest, almost certainly the result of careful attention, but so what? I like a man who takes care of himself. He's a little smaller than I am, a little more slender and ten years younger, but when my hand finally presses against his erection I'm not disappointed. Michaels is just as ready as I am. "Is that what you want? Is this—" I pause and grind my hard-on against his ass, getting a groan out of him, "what you want?"

"I do," Michaels says, "but…"

"We'll be fast," I promise him, already undoing his belt. "No one will walk in on us. We'll be in and out."

"Hopefully not quite that fast," Michaels says, tilting his head toward me with a grin. I smile back, glad to see desire winning out over fear.

"No," I agree, slowly parting his fly. "Not quite that fast." I take him out and stroke him, and he leans back against me and moans. "You feel so good, Matthew. Do you want my mouth or do you want to come from me fucking you?"

"God, just fuck me," Michaels whines. "Fuck me before I fucking come all over this goddamn table without waiting for you." Another thing I like about Michaels: his ability to talk dirty.

He asked for it. I jerk his pants down to his ankles and push him forward onto the table. He spreads his fingers out across the slick, smooth surface of the wood and spreads his feet as far apart as he can, given the restrictions. I undo my own fly and pull my cock out, stroking it with one hand while rubbing the other over Michaels's back. After a minute I reach into my pocket and grab the condom and small tube of lube I'd tucked away earlier. I roll the condom on, slick my cock with the lube and then place both hands on Michaels's hips, lining up. I pause at the entrance to his body, and glance briefly over at the office's bathroom doors. Then I slam inside.

"Motherfucker!" Michaels arches his back, hands slipping on the table's surface as he's driven forward by my thrust. Yet another thing I like about Michaels: he likes it rough. "Give it to me, you bastard, make me feel it, make me fucking scream." Yes, under this accountant's mild-mannered exterior lurks a mouth that puts sailors to shame and an ass that craves cock. I want to make him scream, but I don't want to give away the game either.

"Not too loud," I mutter against his ear as I slowly pull out. I go all the way out, just barely inside him, before driving back in.

It's tight but it feels so good, he's working me with his muscles and goddamn if I don't just want to give in to the temptation, but I can't. "We don't want someone coming to investigate. Can you stay quiet, or"—I thrust again—"do I need to gag you?"

"Oh, fuck," Michaels whimpers. He throws his head back and pushes into my next thrust, meeting me halfway. I don't really want to gag him; I like the noises he makes and, after all, they add to the ambiance I'm going for, but it would be hot. "No," he says finally, "I can handle it."

"Good." He says he can, I believe him. It's not like we're really in any danger, but I want to play it up. I set our pace; a hard, steady rhythm; not terribly fast. I like to watch my cock as it slides in and out of his body, not just as an indistinct blur of motion but so I can see every vein, every twitch. I'm gripping his hips and controlling our movements, and Michaels keeps spouting filth, not loudly but in earnest.

"Jesusfuckingchrist...harder, you fucking bastard, harder, God, I want it, I need your cock...oh, Jesus, fuck me, give it to me, Jake, fucking give it to me...oh, fuckfuck*fuck*—" He's so close to coming, and I haven't even touched his cock. His sweaty hands are making squeaking noises on the table and before long his chest will be against it, he's slid so far.

I think it's time to finish this delightful little interlude. I reach down and wrap my fingers around Michaels's cock, beating it in tempo as I drive into him. He loses his ability to articulate and comes with a strangled cry, his spunk spurting all over the table. He misses his shirt, fortunately. I bury myself as deep as I can inside of him and groan. My body is screaming for release, but I manage to rein it in somehow. It fucking hurts, but I know it'll be worth it.

I bend over Michaels and hold him for a long moment, letting both of us catch our breath before pulling out. "Nice." I grin as

I kiss the back of his neck. "And still so glib."

"Can't help it," Michaels mutters as he straightens with a sigh. "Holy fuck, Jake. I'm going to feel this for a week."

"You're gonna have a good week then, Matthew." I remove the condom as though I've come and somehow tuck myself back into my pants. Michaels is refastening his own and fixing his buttons. Any time now...

The phone rings. The landline.

"Shit." Suddenly Michaels seems to remember where we are. "It's Mr. Brandt's phone."

"It's not like he or Susan are here to answer it," I remind him gently. "Still, probably best to get going. I'll clean up the table, Matthew." The phone stops ringing. I pull him close and kiss him lightly. "You're fantastic, you know that?"

"Yes," he replies impishly, hooking his arms around my waist. He might have said more, but then the phone starts going again. "Fuck. Yeah, okay. I'm out of here. Have a nice time in Tahiti, Jake."

"I will," I say. I watch him leave, and as soon as the door closes I walk over to it and lock it. I head toward the bathroom, grabbing Michaels's forgotten tie as I go, and open the mostly closed door. I flip the light switch. Henry is sitting on the edge of the sink, his cell phone in hand, a smirk on his handsome face.

"You better not have come," he tells me, his voice low and growly and impossibly sexy. My hard-on is going to rip the seams of these pants out any second.

"I didn't," I assure him. I haven't seen Henry in over a week. My eyes linger on the slim, expensive lines of his suit, the distinguished tinges of gray at his temples. The enormous bulge in his pants. A week without Henry is a week too long, especially when he makes me wait for him for release. "You look good."

"You look like a slut," he says, putting the cell phone down.

He stands up and walks over to me, but doesn't touch me yet. "Tie." I give him the tie. "Hands." I extend my hands in front of my body, and he wraps the cloth around them in a fast, effective knot. He grabs me by the leftover length and pulls me into his conference room. We walk back over to the table, and he spins me around, then lifts me and throws me down onto my back. I'm lying in Michaels's cum, and it's making the slippery surface even worse.

Henry jerks my pants off my hips and down my legs. I manage to kick my shoes off before he gets that far, and they fall down together with the pants, a very expensive jumble of clothes. My briefs follow and then I'm lying there, half-nude, hands tied, looking up at my lover of twelve years as he stares down at me. His face is inscrutable, he's wearing his "business expression," but his body is yearning for mine. He reaches a hand between my legs and lightly fingers the plug in my ass. "Good boy." I don't say anything. It isn't my place to speak.

Henry unfastens his own pants, freeing his erection. God, I love looking at him when he's like this, when he's so hard and ready for me from the show that he doesn't want to take the time to undress. I like being fucked by a guy in Armani, go figure. I love being fucked by Henry, and I want him now. My earlier session with Michaels was more for Henry than it was for me, and I'm so ready for him. He sees it and has pity on me. Henry pulls out the plug, sets it on the table next to my head, then reaches in, grabs my hips and plows into me.

And this, I tell myself as I gasp at the intense, burning stretch, is why I wear the plug. Henry is fucking huge. If I didn't wear the plug I wouldn't be able to take him the way he likes. Fortunately we figured that one out early on, and the burning gives way to delicious, aching pleasure in moments. He pulls my legs around his waist and leans his weight down onto me, and I loop my tied hands over his neck. I'm so close. So fucking close, and Henry is pounding into me, sliding me across the table and pulling me back and slamming in again. I look into his eyes and I can see that he's still seeing me fuck Michaels against this table, and it makes him hungry. He's fucking me and it's killing both of us and I've got to fucking come soon or I'm going to die of a goddamn aneurysm, and I'm trying so hard to be quiet but I can't help the plaintive "Henry…" that falls from my lips.

That does it for him. Henry leans in, kisses me brutally, then whispers in my ear, "Come."

Thank god. I let the coiling heat that's been building in me go, finally, and my orgasm is so intense it's blinding. I scream the way I wouldn't let Michaels, my body as tense as my voice as I come and come. My eyes squeeze shut but the world is still swimming, and I can barely breathe. I feel Henry's release inside of me, his hands tightening on my hips until the short nails break the skin. He collapses a little against me until he has regained control, and then he's kissing me again, soothingly. "Jake…" he murmurs against my lips. "Relax, baby." He kisses my forehead and my cheeks and the tip of my nose. I come down from the glorious high, sore and slightly hoarse, and open my eyes. Henry is smiling at me. "Hey, baby."

"Hey."

"Well done." He kisses me again, then slowly pulls out and helps me sit up. As soon as I'm upright he's pulling me into his arms, though, and I happily go there. We're semidressed, covered in spunk and cuddling against a fifteen-foot, hundred-thousand-dollar dick, and it's perfect. "You set the tone with him beautifully. Nice move with the tie. I almost hoped he'd have to be gagged."

"Yeah, but I know how much you like to hear them beg," I say with a grin.

"True. And Mr. Michaels is so enthusiastic about it." He kisses my temple. "He was a good choice."

"Yeah, I like Matthew."

Henry arches his eyebrow. "Really?"

I grin again. "Yes, really. Because he makes you nervous."

"Excited, Jake, there's a difference." Yes, there is, and I can always feel it in his body after he watches me with Michaels. He's rawer, more possessive. Excited yes, but also jealous. I like that I can still make him jealous. "Smugness isn't attractive, Jake."

"Sorry. Are we set to leave?"

"Our bags are down in the car. We can leave immediately, Susan will be in to clean this up later." Susan has worked with Henry even longer than I have, and they have their own special relationship with regard to kink.

I glance at the bathroom. "Should I shower first? I'm kind of gross here."

"There's a shower on the jet. I want to smell you a while longer."

"Pervert," I grin as he unties my hands.

"Cumslut," he replies unrepentantly, as he gives me the tie. It's a fairly nice one. "Are you going to give that back to Mr. Michaels?"

"I think I'll mail it to him from Tahiti."

"And the sentiment?" Henry asks, leaning in and nipping gently at my earlobe. I can already see us in the beach house, in bed, me with my hands tied to the bedposts as my lover gets more and more mileage out of tonight's exhibition.

"Thanks for all the memories."

EXHIBITION BEACH

Jay Starre

Rory was a gorgeous man. In fact, he was so fucking hot nearly everyone was afraid to hit on him or even approach him. That suited him fine, especially when he went to Wreck Beach for his summertime descent into a nasty, naked flaunt-fest.

By the time July rolled around, the rainy days of spring on coastal British Columbia had mostly passed and the long days of the northern summer had commenced. The densely forested slopes that sheltered the clothing-optional Wreck Beach from the city of Vancouver were still moist from those spring rains. And once the sun beat down on them full force, they grew positively steamy.

Steamy too were the hopes of the gay men who frequented the several kilometers of quiet trails away from the busy main beach and its crowds of naked sunbathers. Rory knew exactly which narrow path to follow, exactly where to slip down to a small break in the cottonwood and fir forest and find an isolated opening on the water.

On his first foray away from the main trail he discovered a delightfully pleasant precursor to his day of nastiness. A man stood alone in the dappled shade of an overhanging aspen, totally naked.

The dude leaned forward, hands up over his head and planted on the smooth bole of the tree before him. His bare feet were splayed apart in the soft sand of the beach. His lower body gleamed pale, while his upper body boasted a swirling array of symmetrical tattoos in vibrant red and green.

Buzzed dark hair contrasted with a pair of soft golden eyes and a pursed pink mouth. He'd heard the snap of twigs and branches as Rory approached through the tangled brush that lined and crowded the trail.

He craned his head around and gawked at the incredibly hot stud that had chanced his way. His round face actually flushed and he gasped aloud. Rory halted half a dozen paces away and stood his ground, bright blue eyes roaming up and down the naked form presented for his viewing pleasure.

The dark-haired stranger visibly trembled as he watched Rory assess him. What did those big blue eyes see? How did they judge him? The fat cock that dangled down between the observing redhead's muscular thighs swelled up and rose to half-mast, but otherwise he said nothing, nor made any move to come closer.

The tattooed dude groaned. Fidgeting nervously, he was too intimidated to say anything himself or make a move on the hovering stud who eyed him so keenly. Instead, he began to writhe. Arching his back, he thrust out his lush white butt, saying with his body what he was afraid to utter aloud.

A faint smile curled the corner of Rory's wide mouth. The stranger he watched moaned and wriggled more enthusiastically. His feet spread wider, opening up his deep buttcrack.

Smooth white flesh parted and a crinkled hole appeared.

Rory's cock twitched upright at his crotch. Yet still he made no move toward that slowly squirming ass. The poor dude was growing desperate by this time. He continued to groan and wriggle that enticing can, then made his final bid for the redheaded stud's touch. He reached back and down to cram one of his hands into his own parted asscrack. A thrusting finger found and impaled the pink asshole.

Rory grinned. This was exactly what he wanted to see; exactly what he needed to get his day started! He nodded and winked, then turned and abandoned the grunting, self-fingering stranger to his own devices. As he traipsed his way back to the main trail, he felt no remorse, nor any pity for the eager dude he'd left behind. The guy was hot, and someone else was bound to find him and fall victim to his charms.

Another path descended from the main trail and he took it. This one he recognized, and since it was still before noon, the clearing at its end was likely to be free for the taking. Careful to avoid the tangled blackberry shrubs that lined the trail, he made his way down to the water.

Perfect! The beach faced west, and the sun would bathe it for the remainder of the day. It was only a small opening in the woods, but large enough for his purposes. The best thing about it was the massive log that sprawled down the middle. A narrow sandy beach bordered the log on the water side, and a tangle of smaller beached driftwood logs were scattered across the other side.

He was already naked; he'd stripped down to his sneakers as soon as he'd come down to the main beach. He carried a small pack with his water, snacks, towels, toys and all-important lube. He spread a green beach towel over the smooth bole of the beached log and then draped himself over it.

Ahh. The warm sun beat down on him while a steady breeze wafted in from the sea. On his belly with thighs hugging the side of the log, his jutting butt was exposed to the sun—and to the eyes of any stranger who happened by. A freckled tan over the rest of his muscled body emphasized the creamy-pale smoothness of that hairless can.

A trainer in a gym, he was all sculpted muscle, from his broad shoulders down to his narrow waist, powerful ass, thick thighs and strong calves. Folded under his cheek, his muscular arms bulged.

He was not in any hurry. The warm sun and cool breeze relaxed him while the waves lapping against the beach murmured a rhythmic song that added to the timelessness of the moment.

His first visitor arrived soon enough. The path Rory had taken down to the clearing wasn't the only avenue for approaching hikers. A second trail path snaked its way along the wooded beach through tangled driftwood and muddy reeds. The more adventurous picked their way along it to discover all the secluded spots like Rory's little clearing.

He came from the direction Rory faced. Naked and carrying a pack of his own, he was tall, lean, blond and young. He halted, just as Rory had earlier when confronting a naked man on the beach. He looked Rory in the eye and blinked nervously.

Rory's startling blue orbs gazed back out of a freckled complexion. Ginger eyebrows and a small red goatee accented his wide-spaced eyes, strong nose and generous mouth. A thick mass of red hair was trimmed short around his neat ears.

The tall youth's look faltered as he found himself intimidated by those stunning good looks. Still, he dared to look farther, eyes roaming over that broad back and upthrust ass. Rory offered a small smile, then deliberately closed his eyes and settled into the log beneath him.

This was the deliciously fun part. Eyes closed, he lay quietly and waited. He was fairly sure this young guy would be too shy to actually touch him, which was fine with him. Listening keenly, he just made out the tentative approach of footsteps as the path took the stranger close on his left along the water's edge; very close, only a yard or so away.

Even with the steady breeze rippling through the branches of the woods, he could hear the young dude as he halted beside him, his excited breathing heavy and rapid. Rory grinned, but kept his eyes shut.

His cock stiffened where it lay along the log back down between his thighs. He had a fat cock and big balls, which were displayed perfectly between his splayed thighs. He moved slightly, lifting up his creamy ass and then settling down again. Totally aware of the eyes watching him, he sighed aloud and wriggled again.

He heard the dude spitting, followed by the sound of a slippery palm pumping up and down a stiff cock. His grin broadened as he bathed in the sunlight, the breeze and those hungry, watching eyes.

He knew exactly what to do to really get a rise out of the young watcher. Pulling his thighs forward, he let his asscrack open wider. Then, remaining still, he began to clench and relax his asshole. Talented sphincter muscles clamped, then yawned.

A loud gasp was followed by a groan and then more gasps. The pumping palm slapped furiously, before suddenly stopping. A strained moan clearly informed Rory his victim was shooting.

Perfect! The poor punk spewed a load while he stared at Rory draped naked over a log, asshole quivering.

The blond moved on and Rory relaxed into his half doze, content to await the next victim of his considerable allure. It wasn't long before the next cruising dude came along, again too intimidated to actually reach out and touch the sprawled redhead, but lingering all the same for a good eyeful of that luscious body. Rory lay over his log and drank in the warm sun and the heated stranger's hungry gaze.

Several others followed, each taking a moment or more to look over the gorgeous naked body before moving on in a search for more attainable prey. Rory reveled in their greedy, appraising looks as he settled in over his log and enjoyed the summer heat.

Birds chirped happily in the dense growth. The high wail of a distant tugboat rounding the headland was the only reminder of civilization.

A pair of passersby arrived together. They were bold enough to approach and surround Rory, planting themselves on either side of the log he straddled. By this time, Rory's white butt had grown pink from the sun and tingling warm. He was acutely conscious of his naked cheeks and exposed, vulnerable asshole.

One of the pair was pleasantly chubby, with brooding eyes and a wicked grin surrounded by a dark beard. The other was well built and nervously excited. They were the boldest of the day so far and began jerking off immediately. Facing each other, they stared down at Rory's sprawled back and ass with nasty fascination.

He teased them. Sighing dramatically and squirming lazily over his towel, he pumped his stiffening cock against the log and fluttered his pink, pouting butthole.

"Oh, yeah...goddamn...so fucking hot," the bearded one whispered.

The muscled one whispered back: "Fuck...what a sweet ass...and hole...I'm gonna blow!"

Rory basked in their moaning orgasms. A feeling of conquest accented the warm satisfaction he experienced due to the exquisite attention he'd received so far on that lazy afternoon. They left him reluctantly while he simply waited for more drifters to come upon him.

When this next dude showed up, Rory knew immediately the time had come for more action. He was older than Rory by about a decade, probably in his early forties. More sure of himself, less afraid of rejection and more able to take it in stride, he looked Rory over speculatively, pumped his very large dick into a full-blown boner, grinned boldly and moved in.

He looked good naked, with the lean body of a runner and athletic grace to go with it. A hint of gray in his auburn hair only added to his foxy good looks. Confident and wielding that heavy battering boner, he strode up to Rory and immediately settled in on the log behind him.

There was no idle exchange of wasted words. He bent down to cram his face into that warm, spread ass. As the new arrival's tongue drilled into Rory's asshole, he smiled and opened up to it.

But the feeling of a mouth clamped over his hole, the sensation of stubbled cheeks rubbing against his crack, and the grip of large, competent hands on his butt, as awesome as they were, simply weren't enough. Not today.

He craved more, and he got it. Just as those hungry lips attached to his pink hole began to suck him inside out, the next spectator arrived.

Rory raised his upper body to plant his hands under himself and faced the newcomer. While the auburn-haired dude behind him ate ass with loud slurps, he gazed directly into the wide, almost frightened eyes of a young naked blond who'd halted a few yards in front of him along the beach trail.

He speared the poor young dude with his bright blue eyes. He smiled, gorgeous white teeth surrounded by that ginger goatee. He licked his plump pink lips and then winked.

The slender blond was probably new to the beach cruising scene. He looked both scared and captivated. Rory loved it. He wriggled nastily back into that ravenous mouth, licked his lips lewdly and continued to stare into the young watcher's mesmerized eyes.

When the older dude rose up to mount him, Rory's grin widened and he winked again. A second arrival halted just behind the hypnotized first to enjoy the show.

As the lubed cock gored him, he let out a histrionic grunt and heaved back to accept it. Now, as a third stranger arrived from the path above, Rory took that cock balls-deep and reveled in the awestruck looks of his audience. Behind him, his partner in crime did his best to put on a good show of his own.

He fucked Rory hard and deep, his lean hips slapping against Rory's round, sunburned buttcheeks. Every powerful thrust rocked him forward on the log he straddled. Every time that cock drove into him, he grunted loudly and licked his lips nastily.

A fourth drifter joined them. Rory squirmed over the log as cock pounded his ass. He looked each of the spectators in the eye, one after the other, wagging his tongue, licking his lips, winking and grunting.

He lost himself in the sensation of being fucked and being watched. It was the culmination of a long afternoon of lazy, exquisite prelude that had only now found its climax.

With all eyes on him, and a thick, stiff cock reaming his gut deep, he spewed.

As he rocked over the log in the throes of intense orgasm, he held nothing back. He let them all see what he was feeling, mouth gaping open, eyes rolling up, body wracked with convulsions.

Two of the watchers shot their own loads, as did his auburn-haired fuck partner.

Now it was his turn to be abandoned. They departed, all of them. He sprawled over his log, ass fucked and balls emptied. The sun had swept around to leave him in dappled shade. It had been a good day.

Another passerby approached. He smiled lazily and wriggled his well-fucked ass just enough to tease. Obviously, the day was not quite over yet.

REAR WINDOW

Logan Zachary

The last thing I expected to see that early in the morning was the most perfect ass in the world. A darkly tanned back glistened with water as two pale white muscular orbs flexed and relaxed. Deep dimples winked at me and wished me, "Good Morning, Duluth." Mr. Perfection was clearly visible to me from street level up through the window of his old brownstone.

I hurried up the four flights of stairs from First Street to slip in the back door of Polinsky Rehab Center. I'm an occupational therapist, and my shift started at 7:00 A.M. so that I could help the patients dress before physical, speech and recreational therapy. My new promotion at work forced me to come in earlier. Man, I was glad I did.

Long, hairy, tanned legs started to turn, and I increased my pace to avoid detection. How I wanted to see all of him, but a small part of me didn't want to be caught peeping.

The new conference room—the perfect place to watch him undetected!

I ripped open the door and raced up three more flights of stairs

to the new corner conference room. They had been working for
months remodeling the clinic. Entering the new space, I saw that
indeed the floor-to-ceiling windows overlooked the old brownstone with Mr. Perfection in the flesh. The office door closed
behind me while my eyes scanned the apartment building for
more hot male sexuality before breakfast.

A thick pubic bush with a flash of a fleshy cock took my
breath away. A white cotton towel was wrapped around his
narrow hips as a muscular hand caressed the rising bulge.

My hand rubbed up and down my fly as my arousal grew.
What an amazing view.

His hand tunneled under the towel and worked his erection.
Faster and faster his fist stroked his cock. Thick white cotton
jerked up and down as his legs spread wider. Sculpted hairy legs
and large feet planted on the floor as his towel billowed.

The glass was cool against my forehead as I leaned against
the huge pane. Could he see me? The ceiling light was off, but I
worried my silhouette could be seen against the hall light or the
rising sun.

The towel pulled loose and dropped to the floor, encircling his
feet. His huge penis sprang free as his hand continued working
his shaft. His low-hanging balls swung back and forth.

I licked my lips, imagining how the furry orbs would taste in
my mouth, rolled between my teeth and tongue. Saliva flooded
over my even white teeth, and I swallowed hard.

His testicles rose higher as a glossy wet sheen spread over the
tip of his dick and spread down the thick shaft.

I could almost hear him moan with pleasure. How I wished
my hand were his. How hard I wished I could be down on my
knees, enjoying the pleasures of the flesh—his flesh.

After several more strokes he pumped out a thick, creamy
load that sprayed across the window.

I unzipped, pulled out my engorged flesh and pressed it against the window. The cool glass did little to reduce my arousal. A drop of ooze dotted the tinted pane. I pressed against it, hoping the pressure and cold would help, but Mr. Perfection stood displaying himself full frontal to me, and my balls leapt in my shorts.

I stroked a few times up and down my thick shaft. How I wanted to blow off some steam; how I needed to get to my desk. Horny and hard, or prompt and promoted? Which would win? My finger rounded the swollen head and spread the thick cream over the tender tip. Dipping into the opening, it milked more precum out. My head fell back as I drew the fluid down my eight inches. More started to flow, lubing up my erection. My hand worked it faster, harder.

Then a door slammed, and I pushed my cock back in and zipped up my fly. I adjusted my cock and walked stiffly to my office. It was going to be a long, hard day.

All day the naked image of Mr. Perfection filled my thoughts. How my body wanted to touch, taste, feel, caress and kiss him, every inch of him.

I had just closed my email when the fire alarms shrilled, strobe lights flashed and a woman's voice said, "Code Red, Rehab Center, Code Red, Rehab Center."

That was us!

I raced out of the office and inhaled deeply: no smoke...yet.

The fire alarms strobed and sounded down the halls, as all the doors opened and therapists' heads poked out.

"I don't smell smoke, but I know this is not a drill. It isn't scheduled until next month," I called down the halls.

Joe wheeled his patient's chair into the hall.

"Shouldn't we evacuate to the hospital, get out of this building?"

"Good thinking, Joe. Everyone use the link to move all the patients back to their rooms," I instructed as I walked down the halls. "Everyone move back over to the hospital." I went from the speech therapy rooms down the hall to pediatrics, making sure all the children were moved also. Turning the corner, I went to the newly rehabbed OT kitchen and then continued to the OT clinic. All the occupational therapists had left. Crossing the hall, I saw that the PT gym was empty too, but I still didn't smell any smoke.

Jan, our secretary, waited at the link.

"Everyone is over in the hospital except you," she said.

"Great, close the doors and I'll head downstairs to make sure no one is down there, and then I'll walk the parking ramp to the hospital."

Jan looked concerned, but did as I asked.

I avoided the elevator and headed down the stairs; entering the lower level, I ran down the hall. The door I had entered burst open, and Mr. Perfection strolled in dressed as a fireman. He had an ax over his shoulder and a phone in his hand. The morning sun formed a halo around his body.

"I just entered the building and there are no signs of smoke," he said into the mouthpiece. He saw me heading toward him and asked, "Is everyone out?" His voice was deep and rich.

"Yes, I was just doing a run-through down here."

"Are you sure it's safe?"

"I haven't seen or smelled any smoke."

"Did someone trip an alarm?"

I didn't remember seeing any flipped down as I raced through the building. "I don't believe so."

Mr. Perfection stopped in front of me. I could see he was shirtless under his scorched fireman's jacket. His pants and suspenders appeared hastily pulled on; he also wore boots and helmet.

Was he wearing underwear?

My mouth went dry, and I forced all naked images away.

"The construction guys are working over here, that's the last place I need to check." I grabbed his arm and dragged him after me. Was I afraid he'd disappear? Run away? My arousal made it difficult to walk. I prayed it wouldn't show through the thin gray material.

I pulled open the door to the whirlpool room and saw spraying water. A loose hose flopped across the floor like a snake and sprayed the walls and ceiling. The sprinkler system rained down as well. Two construction guys lay on the floor, soaking wet.

I released Mr. Fireman and headed toward the men. I grabbed one's wet shirt above the shoulders and pulled him across the floor. His body slipped easily over the wet tile. As I looked to the side, I saws that Mr. Fireman had grabbed the other guy and was dragging him alongside of me.

Water poured over me, soaking me instantly. My clothes stuck to me as I fought them, pulling the construction worker out the door. I gently laid him down and ran to the water shutoff valve. I opened the door and Mr. Fireman was right behind me. Together we found the valve and turned it off. He pulled his phone out and spoke into it.

"Looks like the construction workers had too much pressure in the hose and activated the ceiling fire-alarm system and flooded out the whirlpool room. We have two down, looks like knocked out cold, possible head injury, send staff from the Miller-Dwan ER to Polinsky's lower level."

"Copy," a woman's voice said.

As we headed back to the men lying on the floor, firemen, paramedics and a few policemen stormed in, ready for action. The unconscious men were quickly assessed and taken to the ER, as the rest of the building was searched. The other construction workers returned just in time to see their coworkers carried off. They entered the whirlpool room and surveyed the damage.

I stood shivering in my soaking clothes.

Mr. Perfect Fireman found a bath blanket and wrapped it around my shoulders. He rubbed me, trying to warm me up. "Are you okay?" Water dripped off my nose and pooled at his feet.

"I'm fine. Just wet and cold, nothing a hot shower and change of clothing won't fix." I smiled weakly.

"You have quick reflexes and act without thinking—hero mentality, if I ever saw it. Maybe we should head to your office."

I felt my face flush as we started to the stairwell.

"Do you have any dry clothes here?" he asked.

"No. I think I can get a pair of scrubs from the hospital."

His hand grabbed my wet arm and stopped me from entering the stairwell. "Seriously, I just live across the alley, in that brownstone. You can shower and change there. I even have some clothes that will fit you." The heat of his touch warmed me down to my toes, and before I could protest, he said, "I'll have you back before they even miss you." He gently guided me to the exit and pushed the door open. He hurried me through the parking ramp, across the sidewalk and down the stairs to his place.

My heartbeat raced as images of this morning flooded my mind. My chilled flesh couldn't quench the fire in my loins. I could feel myself strain against the wet fabric of my pants and underwear. How I longed for his touch; how I longed to touch him. He opened the door to his apartment and ushered me to the bathroom. He took off the towel and pointed to the shower. "Warm up in there. I'll get you another towel and some dry clothes." He turned on the shower and left.

Slowly, I unbuttoned my shirt and peeled it away from my

skin. I kicked off my shoes and bent over to pull off my socks. I detected some movement and peered between my legs. Mr. Perfection stood there.

"Is everything all right?" his deep, rich voice asked.

I pulled off both socks and stood up. He reached forward to take them. "Did you want me to wash them or just dry them?"

I picked up my shirt from the floor and handed it to him.

"They're clean, just wet."

He stood there, waiting for my pants. My face flushed as I undid my belt and removed it from the loops. I unzipped and slipped the wet fabric down my hairy legs. My pelt matted to my body. My white briefs were almost see-through.

Mr. Perfection kept a cool expression and waited.

I turned my back to him and peeled the second skin from my butt. My erection sprang free and I used one hand to try and cover it. I hid behind my pants and briefs as I tossed them to him. Quickly, I bolted into the hot water of the shower and pulled the curtain closed.

Hot water scalded me, but it felt good to be warm again. My cock grew even longer and harder from the heat. I soaped up quickly and rinsed. I turned off the water and pulled back the shower curtain.

There he was in all his glory. His jacket was open, revealing a bare chest. His pants hung low on his narrow waist. The top button was open and a shadow of thick black hair peeked through the opening. A bulge thrust out just below the opening. He held a thick, fluffy towel for me.

The shower curtain hid my state of arousal. Could I get the towel and still maintain my modesty?

He held the towel just out of reach.

My eyes scanned his torso, caressing every curve line, then worked lower to the dark triangle that seemed to have grown. I looked into his eyes. He smiled and let the towel unfold, daring me to step out.

I pushed the curtain out of the way and stepped into his towel.

His hands wrapped the cotton around me. His fingers caressed the crescents of my ass. My buttcheeks flexed as I waited for him to step back, but he didn't. He stood his ground. His breath was hot on my rapidly cooling body, as the water dripped down me. His jacket slipped off his shoulders and pooled around his ankles.

I reached up and slipped his suspenders off his shoulders. Watching them fall, I prayed gravity would be kind. It was. His bush of pubic hair exploded out of his waistband, and the thick root of his cock followed. I was right, he didn't have underwear on. *Yeah.* His fireman pants hung on his dick and teased me.

I was so close. His show that morning had displayed impressive dimensions from far away; I held my breath now, standing only inches away. I willed his pants to fall. Mr. Perfection took a deep breath and all was revealed, ten inches of manhood. He stepped out of his pants and pulled me closer.

My towel dropped and our flesh dueled.

He guided me to his bedroom and lay down.

I bent forward and licked the huge mushroom head of his dick. Precum already lubed the hole and another pearl ran down the underside. My tongue caught it and drew it back to the tip, circling it around and around, milking more cream out of him.

He threw his head back and brought his legs up.

I worked down his thick shaft and pulled one ball into my mouth. I tried to swallow it, but the low-hanging orb was too fat and full. Releasing it, I kissed his other one and slowly drew it into my mouth. I rolled it between my teeth and he moaned with pleasure. He pulled a pillow down from under his head and slid it under his lower back. His hot ass, pale and pink, spread for me. His tight hole winked at me as the dark hair ran down his crease to form a wreath around his prize. My tongue trailed down his balls, into the crease and circled his hole. I drilled the sweet spot and sought entrance. Mr. Perfection spread his legs wider, opening himself up. His sphincter loosened and allowed my tongue to enter deeper.

"Please," he begged in his deep voice.

I climbed onto the bed and knelt between his legs. My raging hard-on leapt when it saw his bubble-butt. The fleshy muscles were covered with a downy fur and begged to be squeezed, used and abused: I was the man to do it. A condom and a bottle of lube appeared, and I didn't need anything else. I suited up, lubed up and soon filled him up, guiding my erection to his hairy crack and slowly slipping it in. Mr. Perfection pressed down on me, pulling me deeper into him. My balls bounced off his ass as I filled him to the hilt. I pulled out and grabbed the bottle of lube. I poured a palm full and slathered it over his cock. His hips rocked back and forth, humping my fist as I rode his butt. His balls danced along my shaft as I entered him. Mine pounded his ass with each thrust.

He moaned and rocked his pelvis, humping my hand as he pushed down on my cock. Lube and precum dripped down his shaft and soaked his hairy balls. I increased my speed as my balls started to rise. Precum poured out of my dick and washed over my throbbing tip. His ass clamped down on my erection, milking more out as I pulled back, and he relaxed as I plowed back in, producing even more precum.

My breathing came in short, hard bursts.

"I'm...I'm...getting...close," I warned.

"Go...for...it," he panted.

I slammed and rammed for all I was worth. The orgasm

exploded from my balls and ran down my length, filling the condom. Wave after wave of pleasure washed over my body as his cock shot in my palm. Ropes of cum sprayed out of him and slathered my six-pack. Thick cream poured down my treasure trail and through my bush. My whole body tensed as pure bliss overstimulated my nerve endings.

I collapsed on top of Mr. Perfection and lay there, our juices mixing and marinating our bodies. The thick cum slowly slid down his body as my breathing returned to normal. I pushed up and bent over to retrieve my towel.

"Great ass."

I wiped the sweat and semen off my body and started to dress in the clothes he'd put out for me. "I'd better hurry and get back."

Mr. Perfection pushed up from the bed and came to stand in front of me. Cum ran down his tan skin.

"Remember to stop back on your way home."

"Why?" I paused in my dressing.

"To get your clothes back."

"Oh," my smile faded. His finger traced my mouth.

"And I was hoping for a second round."

"Really?"

"I've only been jacking off in my window for the last six months, trying to catch your attention."

"Well, you've got it now."

"Good, and wait until you see my new neighbor. I've enjoyed watching him move in. Maybe we'll see more, together."

I stepped closer and kissed him deeply.

"Or maybe we could *show* him some more..."

A FINAL
GOOD-BYE

Pepper Espinoza

S he told me to be there at midnight, but she didn't tell me why and I didn't ask why she wanted me. I never ask. She told me where to go and what to do, but her instructions weren't specific. It wasn't a request or a demand, just a simple exchange of information. But at the bottom of her email she added *I think you'll like this*. Just the sight of the words made my heart race and my cock twitch. I never told anybody the things I shared with her, and when she said I would like something, she was speaking from a place of authority.

There were so few opportunities to really indulge my desires. Pornography was the most obvious outlet, but it did the job without any satisfaction. While I did have the occasional lover, I never felt comfortable explaining what I wanted and then asking them to please give in to my sick desires. A few of them might have—a few of them really got into kinky shit. But *she* was the only one who figured me out before I ever said a word. *She* was the only one who had the nerve to tease out the truth. She left me in the end, but sometimes she still emails me, still calls me to her. I should have never let her go.

She put me in her closet. I didn't mind, since she'd rather thoughtfully provided a chair, some tissue and some lotion, a bottle of water and a pillow. She left the door partially open, cleverly disguising my presence without blocking my view. She was efficient like that. She told me her guests didn't know about me, and she wasn't going to tell them. I was already half-erect, but that information had me straining against my zipper. It was always better when the people I watched didn't know. I didn't want to see a performance. I didn't want them to be self-conscious or looking over their shoulders every five minutes. I would have been a piece of furniture if I could have been.

She's not a traditionally beautiful woman. When she meets new people, they can always tell there's something a little different about her, though they rarely guess *what* or why she gives them that sense. It wasn't until she got naked and you could see the way all the parts fit together that you realized what set her apart from everybody else. She called herself Katie, but she'd once been Sean, a rather strapping young man with an all-American square jaw. That part of her past never bothered me. Why should it? I rarely even thought about it. Even when she stripped down and I saw the way she kept her cock bound against her thigh, it didn't bother me. I loved her and a part of me always would love her. It killed me to think of her with another man, but that pain winding through my chest only heightened my sexual desire. It made me ache in new ways until I was all twisted up inside, my heart and cock throbbing with equal intensity.

About fifteen minutes after I'd settled in the closet, her two guests arrived. I didn't know either one of them, or their names. I decided to call the taller one John. He had broad shoulders and a deep barrel chest. His arms were huge, and his hands were rough with old scars and oil stains. His head was completely bald, except for a mustache and a thin goatee. A huge tattoo of an eagle covered his back, and his cock was a good eight inches. I called the shorter guy Ted. He was completely normal in every way. He wore jeans and a polo shirt, his haircut was nondescript and he didn't have any tats or visible scars. His watch was nice without being too flashy, and that was his only piece of jewelry. Ted looked like somebody she must have met at work. One of the pencil pushers in middle management who never got beyond middle management and never lost any sleep over that fact. They both looked at her like they could eat her alive.

I had my pants down around my ankles, but I kept my hand off my cock for as long as I could stand it. Just watching the three of them undress was enough to make my cockhead damp with precum. The fluid gathered at the slit and then rolled down my length in long, lazy streams. Sweat rolled down my neck and brow in the same lazy way. I felt every breath and flutter of my pulse. I was completely attuned to my own body the same way they were attuned to hers. Their hands and mouths were all over her flesh, licking at the damp skin on her neck, beneath her arms and on the inside of her thighs. She dropped her head back in obvious ecstasy, and her long hair flowed down her back, creating a curtain that partially obscured Ted's face. It would have been a perfect opportunity to imagine myself in Ted's place, but I didn't want to be there.

They pulled her to the bed and she stretched out in the center, spread-eagle and waiting. John secured her wrists in place, binding her to the bed while his mouth remained on her body. He pulled her nipples between his lips, sucking on them until she arched off the bed, her spine curved, her chest thrust out. Her cock was hard, still strapped to her thigh. Neither of the men paid any attention to it, even though it glistened with precum that would have made anybody's mouth water. Her breath quickened with each hard suck, and her mouth opened and closed in wordless encouragement. Ted took her feet, gently securing her ankles with the Velcro cuffs. Once they were in place, he ran his fingers along the line of her calf, his mouth following his hand. Her skin was smooth and pale. It looked like silk, and it probably felt even better. Her body was always so soft, so perfect, and she smelled like fresh vanilla. That scent surrounded me in the closet, drifting from her clothes, tickling my nose and the back of my throat.

John moved away from her first. He reached under the bed and pulled out the leather case—the one I had never been allowed to open, though I always knew it was there. He unzipped it slowly, prolonging the anticipation until she began to pull impatiently against her cuffs. When he finally pulled the top back, the light overhead caught the blades and reflected back into John's face. I covered my mouth with one hand to muffle the sound of my breathing, but the sight of the knives was almost too much. My other hand rested on my thigh, twitching and eager to finally wrap around my shaft. I imagined the pressure of my own fingers against the throbbing skin, felt every inch of skin touching skin, but stopped myself from taking that step. Not yet. Soon, but not yet.

John studied his options for a moment and then selected one knife with a long, thin, wicked-looking blade. He lifted it from the case reverently, like he was a priest and she was his sacred offering. Ted froze and so did I. We both stared at John with rapt attention, waiting for him to select the spot on her body. He dragged the dull edge of the blade down her chest, between her breasts to her flat stomach. Every time she inhaled, the steel pressed against her flesh, creating a slight indentation. A single motion of his wrist would have buried the blade in her tender

stomach up to the hilt, and even though I knew she'd never put
herself in the hands of someone who'd do that, the danger made
the hair on my neck stand up. A pain settled deep in my groin;
something sharp and throbbing, something I couldn't ignore. I
shifted in my seat, unconsciously trying to relieve the pressure.
My mouth went dry at the same time, but I couldn't pull my
attention from the sight in front of me long enough to find the
bottle of water.

Finally, John turned the blade over and just let the tip rest
against her stomach. She stopped breathing. I stopped breathing.
My gaze was locked on the point where the knife met skin, where
the hard edge of the steel contrasted against her pliable skin.
After an impossibly long second, a perfect ruby drop welled up
from her flesh. It clung to the knife, an unbelievable shade of
red. I licked my lips, entranced as the drop grew fat and then fell
down the side of her skin, painting the pale canvas of her body.
Another followed it. And another. And another. John dragged
the blade up to her breasts, creating a long, shallow cut. With
his eyes locked on hers, he bent his head and lapped up the
ruby drops, catching them with his wide tongue and moaning in
delight at the hot, salty taste.

The blood was so slight at first that I saw every single drop.
I could count them on her body. I could imagine how each one
would taste. But John wasn't shy about using the blade, applying
just enough pressure to draw out more and more blood without
causing her any real harm. Ted knelt beside the bed, slightly
blocking my view of her stomach, and gripped the base of his
cock. I shifted in my seat, craning my head to the side to get a
better view as he dragged the tip of his cock through her blood,
spreading it around her flesh and painting his skin. After the
pink head turned a darker shade of red, he shifted and brought
his cock to her mouth. She opened for him eagerly, accepting his

length between her lips, licking her own blood from the flesh before closing her mouth around him.

That was the moment I lost the last thread of my self-control. I fumbled with the lotion bottle, squirting a good amount over my heated cock before gripping it with desperate fingers. I *wanted* to stroke myself slowly. I wanted to take my time. I wanted to build up the heat and the pressure until I finally erupted in slow flashes. But that wasn't happening. I don't know why I love the sight of blood: real blood flowing over real skin, emerging to join real blades in the midst of real pain. I don't know why she likes it, either. I don't know why she writhed with pleasure instead of jerking away from the blade, and I don't know why she had a look of such bliss as she cleaned her own blood from Ted's skin.

My wrist moved faster and faster, pumping my cock with abandon. I gripped the base with my other hand, squeezing and relaxing my fingers, massaging the sensitive flesh there while my slick palm slid over the roaring nerve endings at the head. That deep ache urged me to move faster and faster, like I could coax the pain out or maybe literally pull it out. More blood covered her skin, and John abandoned the knife, tossing it aside without another thought to drag his palms up and down her torso, spreading the blood over her breasts and down her thighs. It streaked across her skin, looking foreign and horrible, and the ache spread to my balls.

Of the four of us in the room, I could tell she was enjoying herself the most. Her eyes were closed, and she moved her head almost as quickly as I pumped my wrist, letting Ted fuck her face. Invisible strings seemed to attach her flesh to his, and each time John moved his hand, her body seemed to follow him. He bent his head and kissed her stomach and breasts, and when he lifted his head, he looked like he had smeared his mouth with lipstick. John moved lower on the bed, to her milky white thighs, and he began kissing her skin, leaving bloody marks in the shape of his mouth. She spread her legs as much as she could with the ankle cuffs, and after what felt like an eternity, he slid his fingers between her legs. She gasped and twisted her hips, and I could imagine John's thick fingers working deeper and deeper into her ass, stretching her for his monster cock.

I pushed my ass closer to the edge of the chair and reached behind my balls. With my wrist still flying over my cock, I worked two dry fingers into my asshole. It hurt at first, my tight flesh rejecting the intrusion. The pain only sharpened the sense of pleasure spreading through my lower stomach, and I pushed harder, momentarily imagining it was John demanding more than I wanted to give, refusing to take my denials for an answer. Once I had my fingers in place, I just held them there, giving myself a chance to become accustomed to the pressure.

John knelt between her legs, stroking his thick cock as the slick blood began to dry on her and the sheets, fading from red to brown. Ted moaned as she closed her lips around the base of his shaft and swallowed, her throat squeezing around his flesh. John did take the time to lube his cock, but he didn't bother with a condom. I watched, light-headed, as he slid his meat between her asscheeks. It disappeared an inch at a time into her willing body, and her muffled moans filled the room, covering the sound of my own rapid breathing. I wanted to push John out of the way. I wanted to punch him in the face and claim Katie as my own. Did she know? She must have known. Oh, she must have known and maybe she just wanted to torture me. Maybe she wanted to see me suffer the way I wanted to see her pain. As the thought occurred to me, she opened her eyes and looked right past Ted to stare at me.

That's the real problem with my girl. We know each other too well. We know how to hurt each other and we *like* it. I got off on her physical distress, and she wanted to see me cry. I let her go because we were killing each other and we knew it. But I still come running when she's feeling a little mean and I'm feeling a little desperate. The two men used her body like they owned it, and I jerked off like I'd never get another chance, and she and I never stopped staring at each other. I moved my other hand faster, fucking my ass like John fucked hers, creating another tenuous connection between the two of us.

I bit my tongue as the pleasure became too much. I felt it swirling and pulsing inside of me, growing fatter and fatter, until my skin couldn't contain it anymore. It whipped through me, searching for an outlet, an escape. I wanted to shout to relieve the pressure, but I just bit my tongue harder until blood finally filled my mouth and rolled down the back of my throat. The stinging, coppery heat lit the fuse and within seconds, I saw fireworks. The pleasure went off in explosion after explosion, and my cock shot long strings of cum into and over my fist. It landed on the closet door; it coated me, warm and slick, and it didn't stop. I felt like I was coming for hours.

Eventually, exhausted, I reached for the tissue. By the time I had cleaned myself up, John and Ted were both spent as well. They collapsed on the bed, their eyes closed, their arms resting around her protectively. And I understood. If she'd told me, I wouldn't have accepted it, but I couldn't deny what my own eyes were telling me. They weren't strangers, like I'd assumed. They were her lovers.

I was sure she mouthed *Good-bye* as I slunk out of the room. When she didn't email me again, I realized she'd meant it.

ECLIPSE

Dale Chase

My last boyfriend thought my infatuation with the moon was cute. For a while he shared my sky watching and even accompanied me to an astronomy club meeting, but he ultimately revealed a patronizing side that even good sex couldn't offset. So I'm encouraged when Noah, an appealing twentysomething, joins the club, smiles at me and in time reveals that he too loves the moon. There's an immediate pull toward each other, and the fact that he appears four days before a lunar eclipse seems to label us as inevitable. When he accepts my invitation to view the eclipse from my rooftop, I am, well, in heaven. We sit side by side as Professor Arnold Saxbe lectures on recent discoveries by NASA's Kepler space telescope, and I contemplate not the five new fiery hot planets Kepler detected but how I'll dress up the roof to make sex more inviting.

The next night I'm at my telescope viewing my friend the moon, revisiting the craterlet Gassendi with a new tingle of anticipation. My vantage point is a treasure in a big city, a six-story building bordered only on one side by a similar seven-story building that is mostly dark due to the flight of laid-off renters. A few top floor windows are lit but shaded, thus I have a mostly dark serenity. The moon smiles down in confirmation.

On the big night Noah arrives at ten, and only then do I realize I should have asked him to dinner beforehand but it's too late now and besides, this is the important part. Since the telescope isn't needed for an eclipse, I've created a nook next to the cooling tower. Blankets, pillows, picnic basket and wine are carefully arranged. Condoms and lube are tucked into a corner of the basket. As the moon is full there's no need for candles and I like that, as if my friend will be viewing us as we in turn enjoy his hide-and-seek spectacle.

"This is great," Noah enthuses as he discovers my preparations. "Perfect view, and it's so unobstructed—which is amazing in the city."

He tells me he lives in the 'burbs with his parents, how he's high enough in the hills for a fine celestial vantage point and until now considered the city a loss. "I'm so glad I joined the club," he adds.

"Me too."

I open the wine as he peers over the roof's two-foot-high stucco perimeter.

"It's like an island in the sky," he muses.

"I hadn't thought of it that way," I reply, joining him at the edge, handing him a glass of wine.

"Look!" Noah cries and I turn my gaze skyward to see the moon's first penumbral shading.

"No," he says. "Over there."

A seventh-floor window in the next building has Noah's attention. Suddenly and brightly lit and without curtains or shades, it allows clear view within and there, looking toward us as if acknowledging an audience, is a naked man—a buff, glistening, well-hung man.

"Holy shit," I gasp. I take a swig of wine as Noah and I watch the guy pull on his dick until it stands an impressive length.

"Are his walls red?" Noah asks. "Look past him."

"It looks like a red curtain. Maybe it's a porn set."

"Or a guy who likes atmosphere."

"A real showman," I counter. "Oh, man, look at that."

The showman has now turned to present his backside, spreading his legs and running his hands over his ass. He kneads his flesh, then slides a finger up his crack, stopping when he reaches his center. He prods a bit, detours to his mouth for spit and returns to his crack where he points as if taking aim, then guides the digit into his butthole. Hand plastered on his cheek, he finger-fucks himself.

"This is incredible!" Noah says, all but dancing beside me. He finishes his wine, I gulp mine, and as we get refills the showman stops his action and leaves the stage.

"Now what?" I ask, bumping against Noah who bumps me back. "This is too much."

We're side by side, up against each other.

"He can't see us, can he?" Noah asks.

"Nah, he's in the light, we're in the dark. He's playing to the world."

"So where is he?" Noah demands, and I think how Noah's prick must be as hard as mine, and this is almost as much a turn-on as the showman. Then the object of our affection is back with a foot-long rubber cock. This time he stands at a quarter turn so we get a bit of profile as he eases the thing into himself. His other hand is on his cock, and he squirms as he takes the dildo and keeps on taking it. He definitely knows how to stage a show.

"Holy shit! He's got it all!"

Writhing as the prick goes deep, the showman fucks himself in languid splendor, which drives Noah and me around the bend. He unzips, drops his jeans. "I can't take it. Either we fuck or I'm taking a flyer over the edge."

I fetch condom and lube from the picnic basket, get in behind Noah, drop my pants, suit up and then I am there, dick up his ass for the real thing, going at Noah while the showman continues his one-man show.

I'm gonna come way too soon, but who can hold back? Noah is working his cock like mad, all of us picking up speed including the showman who is now ramming the dildo home and stroking his big dick. It's like some wild animal fuck, and then I'm there and I'm shouting which I almost never do, and I look over and see the showman arching as he unloads. Noah is yelling that he's coming, and I'm thinking about his jizz going over the side, raining down on passersby, which only adds to the fun. Fuck city. Fucking fuck city.

At last we're empty, and I slide out of Noah but wrap my arms around him, running a hand up under his shirt to tweak a tit. "Man, that was something," I say, nuzzling his neck, but he doesn't reply because he's fixed on the showman who you'd think would take a break but now has company. He is kneeling to suck the dick of a naked blond guy who has suddenly appeared. "I can't believe this," I manage, and Noah starts to laugh.

"Porn city," he says. "Let's get naked too."

As we strip, I have a one-second stab of concern at getting naked on my roof but how can we not, what with the show across the way? The cozy sex nook I'd prepared looks silly in the face of the showman's extravaganza. Noah and I embrace, kiss and play grab-ass for maybe a minute before we get more wine and go back to the edge.

The blond is a lanky sort, tall and slim, and his cock is much the same. The showman rubs it over his face before sucking it like a lollipop, then deep-throating the whole thing. "Whoa," Noah says, almost choking on his wine.

"I'd suck your dick," I tell him, "but I don't want to miss this."

He guides my hand to his prick, which is up again, and I work him while the blond across the way plays with his own tits as he's blown by an expert.

"Let's get more comfortable," Noah suggests. "Bring the blankets over here." We drag our nest to the roof's edge, even the picnic basket, and as we settle in we find we can play with each other while still watching the show. Noah climbs into my lap, and my hard dick runs up his crack as we see the showman finish his meal and stand. "Fuck time!" Noah cries and he's right. The showman bends, spreads and the blond takes aim, guiding his prick toward the waiting ass like a pilot coming in for a landing.

"Do me," Noah says, squirming in my lap, so I push him off long enough to suit up again, then ease him back down onto me but this time with my dick up his chute. He gently rides me as the blond gives us a total fuck show. Like the showman, the blond plays to the world, pulling out his dick and waving it around like a fire hose before easing it back into the showman, who squirms a welcome. So we are like this, fucking and watching for I don't know how long, when the blond suddenly pulls out, flips the showman around, pushes him down and sprays come onto his face. The showman's tongue is out; he's trying to catch the spray, and I can't help but give it to Noah because this is just too much. I push him off me and onto all fours, then go back up him and ride his ass to a major come, all the while watching the show across the way.

"I can't see!" Noah complains as I ram it home.

"He's sucking dick," I say only when I'm spent. I pull out

and Noah rights himself. We both peer over the edge to see the blond's cock now at rest yet still impressive. And then, as if we're not already in heaven, a black man steps into the picture. Naked, of course.

"Holy shit!"

"This has to be a porn set," I say, but Noah disagrees.

"Where are the lights, the crew? No, these guys are just into their own little show."

"Little?" I say, kissing him, but neither of us can keep away from the showman's window so we cuddle up for the third act, wondering how many more guys are waiting in the wings.

The black guy is totally ripped, oiled and ready to go. His prick is a thick purplish red, and he's got the showman and the blond on their knees before him, shoving into one mouth, then the other, taking just a couple of strokes before changing.

"The blond's pulling the showman's dick," Noah says, leaning forward as if he can get closer. "Look."

Sure enough, while mouths are engaged, hands and cocks are too, but pretty soon that changes as the black guy turns them around, runs his finger up each butthole simultaneously, works them a bit, then starts to do a serial fuck, one then the other as the showman and the blond bend to present their asses. I start to play with Noah's cock and he with mine, and soon he's got a finger in me.

"This is better than porn," he offers as we watch the fuck show. The black guy takes it slow, keeps at his two partners like he can go all night, and we're hoping he can because we'll be there with him. Then, when he's got his men totally squirming, he stops the action and moves offstage.

"What now?" we say together, which makes us laugh.

The black guy returns with some kind of leather contraption that he fits in the blond's mouth and over his head. It's a series of straps with what appear to be reins. "It's a bridle," I say to Noah and he agrees. "He's going to ride him!"

When the black guy gets his dick back into the blond and starts to thrust, we see he's got a small whip and he slaps his horse on the leg and yanks back on the reins.

"Horsie!" Noah cries.

What's amazing is how the black guy's posture changes. He's more upright as he fucks, like he's some English dude riding with hounds.

"It's a canter," I offer and Noah agrees.

"Yeah, he's in the saddle." The guy goes easy, like he's ready for a long ride, and we are in total awe. "Right here on your roof," Noah adds, like we're part of their action.

"Where's the showman?" I ask because he's been off stage too long. Noah prods my bunghole and I gasp. "Then again, who cares? Are you going to fuck me?"

"You better believe it," Noah says. As horse and rider canter across the way, we reposition so I'm on all fours facing the action, Noah behind me, easing in.

"Ride me, cowboy," I tell him.

"Yee-haw!" he cries just as the showman returns to the scene. He's now clad in a leather harness that stretches across his chest and has reins looped around his back. We watch as he takes his instructions, then gets in front of the blond, eases back against him, bends and spreads to allow the blond's very stiff prick up his butt. The reins are then looped around the blond so the black guy has both sets. "Hey, a fuck train!" Noah says and rams his cock into me in answer.

The three set up a good rhythm and it's obvious they're well practiced, unlike Noah and me, who are veritable babes in comparison. But that doesn't lessen the pleasure because there is nothing quite like watching live porn while fucking, and

Noah's got a sweet dick and a jabbing stroke that is sending jolts through my entire lower region.

The black guy enjoys a long ride, then finally starts to whip his ponies in earnest, yanking on the reins, and we can see he's in full gallop now. "He's there!" Noah shouts as the rider puts his head back, stops whipping but keeps up a mighty thrusting while the blond attempts to stay connected to the showman. I envision a veritable sea of come.

At last the threesome is over and everyone disengages except Noah and me.

"You think they're done?" he asks.

"No way."

Leather gear is discarded as is the whip. The showman and blond each suck a tit on the black guy's formidable chest while he stands with hands on hips. After a bit, the blond steps away while the showman climbs the black guy who then turns him upside down like he's the strongest guy in the world, looping the showman's legs over his shoulders to get at his butt. And then what does he do but dive in. He seems the most limber guy in the world as he arches just enough to get his face into the cheeks. We can only imagine a snake of a tongue drilling the pucker.

Meanwhile, the blond is back, crawling between the black guy's legs with a rubber cock which he shoves into the show-man's mouth so they're all engaged again, and Noah starts to madly thrust into me because who can hold back with that show going on. He slaps my ass as he pumps out his load.

Noah and I then collapse on our blankets, but the action across the way doesn't stop. When the fanny feast is over and the actors take a short break for bottled water, we try to guess what's next.

"He'll have them suck each other," Noah ventures but I counter with, "No, fuck each other. He's into that."

We are both wrong, of course. What is brought onstage next is a two-headed dildo that has to be a good three feet long. The showman and the blond are made to lick the ends, drawing the thing into their eager mouths, lapping the respective knobs until they shine. They then turn and bend while their black master tethers them on the thing, ass to ass, then begins an easy thrust back and forth, fucking them both while his own impressive piece of meat remains soft.

"Maybe he's done," I say.

"No way. Just give him time."

We drink the last of our wine, loose now from hours of sex and drink. The night air adds to the pleasure, having failed to cool down as expected—or maybe that's just us in our hothouse sex grotto. We enjoy more leisurely play as the black guy's big cock slowly fills. He gradually moves the two men closer together so each takes more of the dildo, until he's got a good foot up both of them. They keep looking back as if to say it's too much, but we doubt they're complaining. I'm cuddled against Noah, enjoying the show and thinking how this is the most unbelievable night of my life, when it occurs to me that there is another show in progress. I look up at the moon and see that it's in partial eclipse, and it's not the initial partial, it's the fading partial. We've missed the total entirely.

"Hey," I say to Noah. "We missed the eclipse."

He turns his head to glance at the moon.

"Guess so," he says, turning back to the action. I gaze upon my celestial friend one more time, finding the familiar smile emerging as the dark crescent fades. He'll understand us missing his show in favor of the one down here. And hey, maybe he's been watching too.

COMPERSION

Xan West

It's called compersion. A dyke friend who teaches classes on open relationships taught me the word for it. Compersion: it even sounds dirty. She said that the kind I do is called erotic compersion, when you get off on watching your partner fuck someone else. I'm not just a voyeur, I don't get off in nearly the same way watching strangers go at it, but when I watch Abe bottom, I get this intense charge. It's one of the quickest ways to get me hard, and he knows it.

He calls it showing off for Daddy. He likes to show off for me. It gives him the opportunity to make me proud and get me off, all at once. He picks tops who are wired like me to get off on tears, fear, control and pain. He does it because he loves to play that way, but also, particularly, because he knows that it will give me a good show. He knows that watching him cry as he gets fucked is sure to make me come.

He had a special treat for me that night; he had been putting it together for weeks. He set up my favorite chair, my Daddy chair, so that I could see everything. He had even thoughtfully provided a footstool, toilet and cum rag in the form of Sam, a boy who I had been hot for ever since I met him three years ago. Sam was in service to a couple, Marcus and Franklin, who always topped together. Abe had been lusting after them for as long as I had been eyeing Sam. He could not hide his cat-got-the-cream grin as he showed them around. He wore his eagerness openly, and I wondered if they were thinking what I would be thinking—about slapping it off his face. I settled into my chair, ordered Sam into position and put my boots up, resting them on his bare back. It was going to be a good night, I could feel it.

Marcus and Franklin cornered Abe against the wall, knives in hand, speaking softly to him. I couldn't hear what they were saying, but his eyes got wider and he had stopped breathing for a moment. He was scared, I could tell from across the room, and just watching the fear on his face made my dick hard. Marcus had a gloved hand on Abe's throat, a knife against his cheek, holding him still against the wall, as Franklin swiftly shredded his clothes from his body.

He was trying so hard to be perfectly still, but I could see him trembling slightly. Franklin's knife toyed with his cock, as Marcus murmured something that made him wince and close his eyes. The moment seemed to last a very long time: the sight of that thick, long, shiny blade caressing his dick. He began to breathe rapidly, his fists clenching as he fought to stay still. It was delicious.

They yanked him away from the wall and stood him between them. He was staring into Franklin's eyes when Marcus punched him on his back. Franklin responded by punching his pecs, and they worked a call and response rhythm together on his body, building it, until it was so fast he had no time to process it. He was struggling, shaking his head and stomping, trying to take

it, but I knew it was too much too fast, and he didn't know
how. That was the point, to throw him off, not let him find his
footing, and I could see it getting to him.

Franklin spun him around, and began pounding into his back
with his fists, as Marcus removed his gloves to put others on. I
knew what these must be—SAP gloves. So did Abe, because he
growled, as Marcus began to punch his chest. I could see him
struggle with it, watched it blossom on his face. He couldn't stop
them, was overwhelmed and off kilter, and he always cries when
you punch his chest—it's like a release valve, and this time I got
to watch it happening and savor each moment.

It was glorious to sit back and watch him struggle against
tears, until he released them. It made my cock throb. When I
saw Marcus continue to pound his chest with punches while
he cried, grinning all the while; saw Abe register that it wasn't
going to stop, and he really could let go, my heart filled up with
love for him. My boy was beautiful when he cried.

Marcus began to ram his fists into Abe's thighs, and his knees
began to buckle. I knew what they were doing. Franklin kept
hitting him in the back of the thighs, while Marcus slammed
him from the front, and then they took him down to the floor,
gracefully, quickly, in this gorgeously coordinated move that
ended with Franklin's boot on his throat and Marcus's knee on
his cock. They paused and smiled at each other, as Abe whim-
pered. My entire focus was on that boot trapping his throat, and
I groaned and dug my boot heel into Sam's back.

Franklin held him in place by the throat as Marcus stood and
began to stomp on his thighs, grinding his boot in, grinning as
Abe moaned, then placing his boot on Abe's cock and twisting it
in. It was brutal and perfect, and I mimicked his movements on
Sam's ass. Then Marcus was holding him in place by the boot
on his cock as Franklin began to kick his arms, and I could see

Abe start to panic, breathing hard, as he realized how ruthless they really were, how helpless he was. The fear filled the air, and I soaked it in, grinding my boot into the bruises I had already put on Sam's ass, savoring it.

They worked so well together; it was as if it were choreographed, the way they moved and connected through him. He was a conduit for their energy. Marcus would thrust his sadism into Abe, and Franklin would drink it down and meet it with his own.

The more they played, the more intense it got for Abe, and it was amazing to watch him struggle with himself to take it, to stay there, to surrender to it. Marcus sat in a chair and pulled Abe onto his lap, holding his thighs apart. Franklin stood over Abe, attached clover clamps to his nipples and pulled the chain taut, stretching it into Abe's mouth. Then he pulled out a cane and made it whistle through the air, watching Abe flinch. He hates canes and loves them, all at once. They don't let him float; he has to push himself to take them every time. That's always been part of the fun for me, playing with pain that creates such struggle, such strong reactions. This was going to be good.

Franklin didn't believe in warm-up. He was known for it. If you were going to play with him, you just had to accept that. So it was no surprise that he didn't start light. The rattan drove into Abe's inner thighs, as Marcus held them in place and groaned, feeling Abe wriggle on his cock. Abe growled around the chain clamped in his teeth and kept on growling as Franklin tore into him with the cane, laying lines of brutality into his inner thighs, moving closer and closer to his cock, relentless, determined. I could see the feral desire in his eyes as he sliced into him, and I knew he was not holding back. One of my favorite things to do with Abe is sit him on my lap and hurt him. He wriggles and squirms deliciously, and it feels just perfect to hold him to me and savor what pain does to him. Marcus was having a good time with it, grinning, gripping my boy, opening his thighs for Franklin, groaning as Abe's ass responded to the cane strokes. My boy's dick jumped with every cane stroke, like it wanted attention, and I could not take my eyes off its jumping.

Franklin noticed it too. He murmured to Marcus and pulled Abe up off of his lap. Marcus had a wicked smile on his face as he bent over the bed, his ass framed by the chaps, glancing over his shoulder at Abe, whose eyes widened. They were going to use his cock. Franklin slid a rubber onto it and stroked it with lube, watching it dance in his hand, before putting on the cock ring.

Abe's cock is one of his best features, thick and curved in just the right way, and oh, does he know how to use it. Franklin slid three fingers into Marcus, widening him, and then gestured to Abe. He told him that he had better stay hard for as long as Marcus wanted to get fucked; that he should settle in for a good long ride, because Marcus was going to need to get fucked for a very long time.

My boy did me proud, sliding in, taking his time, twisting his hips just right, as Marcus groaned. He pumped him real slow, groaning around the chain between his teeth. I could see his sore thighs rubbing against Marcus, watched him wince as he hit the welts, but it did not stop him from focusing on the fuck. He is so hot when his cock is being used. It brings him into himself, straightens his shoulders, stirs his pride. He knows he is skilled at this.

My boy is attentive and focused. It's not about his pleasure, it's about you, and he is so focused on you that you feel larger, immense, like you fill the entire room. Abe only wants to give you what you need, to create the kinds of sensations you most enjoy, and he pays such close attention. His gaze and focus is a mighty thing, and as I watched him turn it to Marcus, watched him serve in this particular way, I filled with pride that he was mine. It made my dick throb, watching him steadily piston Marcus—it was intensely hot, but it also lit me up to watch him take such pride in his service. *That's my boy,* I kept thinking. *That's my boy.*

Marcus was telling him how to do it, to stay deeper in, to ram his cock into him in short spurts, never pulling it all the way out; that it felt so good he didn't want it gone for even a second. Abe did as ordered—of course—groaning, and then he jumped a little, as he heard Franklin yank his belt out and snap it.

I could almost feel the belt in my hands as I watched him. Belts are my favorite thing to use on Abe. I am a Daddy, after all. There is nothing like ramming into him with my belt. It's the closest thing to fucking him. Hell, I often end up fucking him as I beat him with it. I love hitting his back with it especially, laying deep bruises into him, but Franklin wasn't hitting him there. He was going after his ass, and I applauded his choice in this case. What could be better than beating his ass as he fucked Marcus? He was using those muscles, which only meant it was going to hurt more, and his ass would look amazing as it purpled with bruises. Abe was screaming, and his screams wrapped around my cock. My dick was throbbing so much I had to stroke it. I pulled it out, grinding my boots into Sam as I stroked, until his groans mixed with Abe's screams and Marcus's moaning, and was that Franklin growling or was it me?

The energy just kept building as I watched Abe sobbing and screaming, pounding into Marcus, his head shaking no, and Franklin just kept beating him with the belt, telling him to take it, to prove himself, that he knew Abe could do it and not to forget to fuck Marcus with all his might.

Sam was whimpering under my boots, and my cock was so fucking hard it hurt. Franklin paused, bent over, put his bag on the bed, yanked his cock out and covered it, sliding a thin layer of lube onto it before ramming it into Abe's ass in one stroke. Abe began to sob, dropping the chain as Franklin fucked him into Marcus, slamming them both into the bed. He reached around to remove the clamps and Abe yowled as they were twisted off, writhing and gripping the bed with his fists until his voice broke, and he began to sob harder. My cock felt like it was going to burst at the sound of it.

I love it when he cries. There is nothing that makes my cock throb more than hearing him sob. And to get to watch it, to hear it, gave me more time to savor the sounds, more freedom to sink into my skin and enjoy it. I didn't have to control myself with him and make sure his sobs didn't ramp me up too high. I could trust that Marcus and Franklin were going to keep up their cruelty, and he would be free to sob as he fucked Marcus; that Franklin would continue to fuck the tears out of him.

This is what I love about watching him: the freedom to let go and really enjoy the impact his tears have on me. That is the show Daddy really wants, and he knows it. This time it was almost too much, the intensity was so high. Abe let out a long choking sob that made me spurt all over Sam. I rubbed myself into his skin and hair, groaning as Sam began to cry, softly. His tears made me spurt more, and I told him so, insisting that he was my cum rag for the night, and I might need to use him again, so he better get used to the feel of my cum on his skin. I pulled him up to face me and told him to open his mouth. I always have to piss after I cum, and there he was, a toilet for me to use. I told him so, insisted he take my piss and swallow it down; that was what he was here for, to be my footrest, my cum rag and my toilet. He sobbed around my cock as he took my piss, and I groaned, opening my eyes and focusing on the scene before me.

Franklin was speaking just loudly enough for me to hear as he rustled around looking for something in his bag. Then there was the smell of alcohol being rubbed on Abe's back, and he went still and quiet. Oh. They were going to push him farther. Abe was afraid of needles and had not played with them before. He had picked two men who loved piercing, and he knew it could happen—he had agreed. His head began to shake as he listened to Franklin, his hands gripping the bed tightly. Franklin was describing how needles were like sex, as he thrust his cock into Abe's ass, slowly, in cadence with his speech. He explained that the reason he loved them so much was that he could create holes in a boy's body, and fuck them. He explained that needle play was about fucking skin, and Abe was so hot that Franklin wanted to fuck him in all the ways he could at the same time. In his ass, his mind and his skin.

Abe began to say, "No, please, no," as he started breathing more rapidly. Marcus reached back and grabbed his wrists, holding them to his own chest. Abe began to cry while he pleaded, "No, please, no," and Franklin laid out the needles so Abe could see them, explaining that the smallest numbers were the thickest, and he wanted a properly thick one to fuck Abe with. I could smell his fear from here; it was palpable, and it made me growl. I pushed Sam onto his back and dug my boots into his cock, twisting them, tasting the fear in the air and the sound of Sam's tears. It was a glorious sound, perfect, the pleading refusal wrapping into the soft tears, and my cock began to stir again.

Abe clamped his mouth shut, and I knew he was on the edge of safewording. His eyes were screwed shut, and he went completely still as Franklin ground his dick into his ass, paused, then thrust a needle into his flesh; into, and through, the point gleaming as it emerged out the other side. My boy trembled, his teeth clenched, fear rising in his chest. Franklin thrust five more needles into him, making a quick job of it, tucking the points into his skin. He was trembling the whole time, barely holding his mouth closed.

I was so proud of him, proud and ravenous for him all at once. Such beautiful fear: it soaked my cock, teasing it, to watch him take those needles. Franklin began to fuck him then, hard, relentless, slamming him into Marcus, talking all the while about how good it felt to fuck his skin, tapping the needles as he spoke, enjoying the way Abe would jump and whimper when he did, never letting him stop thinking about the piercings in his back. Abe began to cry, to say he couldn't take it anymore, please get them out, he just couldn't do it, and Franklin insisted that he better fucking take it until he made Marcus come.

My boy wailed, "No!" at that, a long helpless sound that hardened my cock till it almost hurt, it ached so much. Abe was sobbing and shaking his head as he began to focus on fucking Marcus, staying with Franklin as he fucked him, matching his rhythm. He rammed him in circular motions, and I could hear Marcus's moans increase until they were louder than Abe's sobbing. Abe began a litany of begging, pleading with Marcus to come; saying how much he wanted to please him, please use his cock, he was so grateful to be used, it was exactly what he needed, to be used up until there was nothing left, he had surrendered it all into their hands, please take everything. Marcus began to growl and thrust his ass toward Abe, and Franklin started twisting his needles, fucking them in and out, telling him he was such a good hole. The whole scene was building, and Abe's desperate begging tugged at my balls and stroked my cock, and I began rubbing it into Sam's bristly hair, groaning at the feel of his buzz cut on my dick. I could smell the blood and the fear and even taste the metal in the back of my throat, and I held Sam's head exactly where I wanted it, stroking myself with his hair precisely as I needed and telling him he was there for me to use him, and he had to take it.

Abe was sobbing now, begging through tears, and Marcus was moaning louder, ramming down into the bed, coming. Franklin was as good as his word, and began taking the needles out, groaning as blood rippled down Abe's back and down his sides onto Marcus. The sight of the blood made me come again, watching that blood slide along his skin; hearing Abe sob intensely, begging Franklin to fuck his ass, to take his hole, to use him as he saw fit. Franklin growled and began to ram him so fucking fast that I was amazed he had that kind of stamina this late in the scene. He snarled at Abe while he fucked him, telling him to be a good hole for him, give it all to him; ramming him so hard that the bed began to really shake, until he released a long moan and stopped, embedded in him, still.

Abe was crying and thanking him, trembling, as Franklin cleaned his back up and bandaged it. He looked spent, like he had given it all and had nothing left, as they pulled him into their arms, holding him close. Sam glanced up at me, and I told him to stay there and take it, and I pissed on his chest and face. His eyes were serene as he swallowed the piss that made it into his mouth. I told him to sit up and look at them, and I rested my boots on his thighs. He sighed softly when he saw them and settled into this new position, my boots resting on him, my cum caked on his skin and soaked in his hair.

Abe glanced up at me and saw me looking at him. His face glowed, and he lit up with pride when I smiled. He knew he had put on a good show for Daddy, exactly the kind of show I might want to join in the second act. After all, Abe's cock was still hard and ready to be used again. Daddy wouldn't want to let that go to waste, would he?

ABOUT THE AUTHORS

SHANE ALLISON is the editor of *Hot Cops, Backdraft, College Boys, Hard Working Men, Black Fire* and *Homo Thugs* and has had stories published in many anthologies. His works include *I Want to Eat Chinese Food Off Your Ass, Eros in a Tearoom* and a volume of poetry, *Slut Machine*.

MICHAEL BRACKEN's short fiction has appeared in *Best Gay Romance 2010, Biker Boys, Country Boys, Freshmen, Homo Thugs, Hot Blood, The Mammoth Book of Best New Erotica 4, Men, Muscle Men, Skater Boys, Teammates, Ultimate Gay Erotica 2006* and many other anthologies and periodicals.

DALE CHASE has written male erotica for over a decade, most recently published in *Bears in the Wild* and *Time Well Bent* and is the author of *If The Spirit Moves You: Ghostly Gay Erotica*. Check her out at dalechasestrokes.com.

MARTIN DELACROIX writes novels, novellas and short fiction. His stories have appeared in a dozen erotic anthologies. He has published two novellas: *Maui* and *Love Quest*. He resides on a barrier island on Florida's Gulf Coast. Visit his blog at martindelacroix.wordpress.com.

PEPPER ESPINOZA works full time as an author and part-time as a college instructor. She has published with Amber Quill Press, Liquid Silver Books and Samhain Publishing. You can find more information about her work at pepperverse.net.

As a former Navy boatswain's mate and merchant marine, **HARLEY JACKSON** has spent many shoreside nights in sailor's hotels, including one that was the inspiration for this story. He claims his discharge for homosexuality was "a masterpiece of understatement." Today, he lives and writes in San Francisco's Tenderloin.

MARK JAMES is a writer of gay erotica with several published short stories and two published novels, *The Iron Hand* and *Escape From Purgatory*. He resides in Dallas, where he is currently working on *Razor's Edge*, the sequel to *The Iron Hand*.

JEFF MANN has published two collections of poetry, *Bones Washed with Wine* and *On the Tongue*; a memoir, *Loving Mountains, Loving Men*; a book of personal essays, *Edge*; and a volume of short fiction, *A History of Barbed Wire*. He teaches creative writing at Virginia Tech in Blacksburg, Virginia.

WAYNE MANSFIELD lives in Perth, Western Australia. He has written many erotic stories for gay men that have appeared both online and in print. More recently he has been writing gay vampire erotica. For more information on Wayne or his published stories, check out his blog at myspace.com/darkness-gathers.

GREGORY L. NORRIS is a full-time professional writer, with work published routinely in national magazines and fiction anthologies. A onetime screenwriter on the fifth live-action *Star Trek* series, "Voyager," he is author of the handbook to all things Sunnydale, *The Q Guide to Buffy the Vampire Slayer.*

ROB ROSEN, author of the novels *Sparkle: The Queerest Book You'll Ever Love* and *Divas Las Vegas,* has contributed to more than ninety anthologies. Please visit him at therobrosen.com.

SIMON SHEPPARD is the author of *Hotter Than Hell and Other Stories, In Deep, Kinkorama, Sex Parties 101* and the forthcoming *Sodomy!* He's also the editor of the Lambda Award–winning *Homosex: Sixty Years of Gay Erotica* and *Leathermen,* and his work has been published in over 300 anthologies. He hangs out at simonsheppard.com.

Residing on English Bay in Vancouver, Canada, **JAY STARRE's** work has appeared in *Best Gay Romance 2008, Best Gay Bondage, Bears, Surfer Boys, Special Forces* and *Biker Boys,* all from Cleis Press. He is the author of two historical gay novels, *The Erotic Tales of the Knights Templars* and *The Lusty Adventures of the Knossos Prince.*

XAN WEST is the pseudonym of an NYC BDSM/sex educator and writer whose erotica can be found in *Best Gay Erotica 2009, Best SM Erotica Volume 2 & 3, Hurts So Good, Love at*

First Sting, Leathermen, Men on the Edge, Backdraft, Frenzy, DADDIES and *Biker Boys.* Contact Xan at Xan_West@yahoo. com.

CARI Z is a Colorado girl who loves snow and sunshine. She's currently living in Western Africa, where she gets a lot of one of those things and absolutely none of the other. Eventually she'll come to terms with it. Until then she sits in front of her fridge and sighs.

LOGAN ZACHARY lives in Minneapolis, MN. His stories appear in *Hard Hats, Taken By Force, Boys Caught in the Act, Ride Me Cowboy, Service with a Smile, Surfer Boys, Ultimate Gay Erotica 2009, Time Travel Sex, Best Gay Erotica 2009, Biker Boys, Unmasked II, Unwrapped* and *College Boys.* He can be reached at LoganZachary2002@yahoo.com.